Dead Heat

Richard S. Prather

AN [*e-reads*] BOOK
New York, NY

:

Copyright, ©, 1963, by Richard S. Prather.
Copyright renewed 1991 by Richard S. Prather
First e-reads publication 2002
www.e-reads.com
ISBN 0-7592-2634-2

For
Scott Meredith
agent, friend, wizard

Other works by Richard Prather
also available in e-reads editions

Table of Contents

One

She had eyes that sizzled and lips like flaming puckers, and a body flaunting the vital statistics you'd expect on a gal with such facial sizzle and smack, but she was not so bright she would give a dummy an inferiority complex. That was the kick in the pants — my pants, of course, since I was with her.

O.K., so she was not an intellectual giant. But when a lovely is medium tall and *not* medium in curve and flow and swoop and zip of thigh and waist and breast and all that, and when she has long thick rust-blond hair the color of falling leaves in autumn, and a walk that can sprain male eyeballs at twenty paces, and her hand is resting gently on your knee taking the press out of your trousers, do you go around looking for intellectual giants?

Not if you're Shell Scott, you don't. And I'm Shell Scott.

I'm a private detective. I am the president, vice-president, secretary, janitor, legman — yeah, I'm that, all right — of Sheldon Scott, Investigations; and, believe it or not, friends, I was working.

Yes, it was at least conceivable that at any moment murder might strike, blood might splatter, mayhem of some sort commence, but with Doody — that was her dopey name, Doody — snuggling chummily next to my right hip, the one in which I'd been shot last night, it was the kind of work that could make play pall on a man.

We, Doody and I, were at the races — along with fifty thousand other Southern California citizens.

Specifically, we were at Hollywood Park in Inglewood, near my stamping ground, Los Angeles, this being the thirteenth racing day of Hollypark's current fifty-five-day meeting. It was Saturday, the twenty-fifth day of a balmy May, a gorgeous afternoon, with just a little crispness in the air but the sun bright and sky clear.

Down on the furrowed track the bugler, resplendent in scarlet jacket and straw hat, raised his long silver trumpet and tooted, and the horses filed onto the track for the first race. As the horses began the parade to the post, the talk and laughter around us, like a constant hum of pleasant electricity in the air, increased a little, rose and fell like a surf of breath and voices.

Well, with all that — and with the jockeys' bright silks adding even more brilliant color to the green of the infield, the massed banks of purple and gold and white flowers, the graceful palms and lakes rippled by slowly swimming white and black swans — and with Doody so close, I would have been enjoying myself immensely except for the nearness of that "work" I mentioned.

Doody and I were on the second floor of the Clubhouse, seated in the block of reserved or loge seats to the right of Aisle 2, past the finish line. Below us and also to our left were the choice boxes overlooking the saddling paddock and walking ring, most of them occupied by well-to-do racegoers, a few owners and officials, well-dressed men and women, most of them very nice people. But I was interested in some not-very-nice people.

They were seated to our left, closer to the finish line, and in the back row of boxes. Three of them: a large lump of beef and muscle named Axel Scalzo; plus his solid shadow, Hale, a sleepy-eyed, slow-moving killer, slow-moving, that is, unless moving a gun or sap; and a second gun-toting friend and bodyguard of Scalzo's known to me only as Deke. Scalzo was the reason I was here at the track — Scalzo and another man, who hadn't yet shown up.

I didn't think the three slobs had spotted me yet. Which probably meant they hadn't looked this way very often or carefully, since there are two hundred and six pounds of me, and with my six-foot-two topped by inch-long white hair stabbing skyward like solid shafts of static electricity, and the equally white and obtrusive brows below that hairline as if a couple chunks of the static had slipped down over my gray eyes, those apes would not, once having seen me before, be likely to confuse me with ten other people.

And they had, all of them, seen me before. We had, as the phrase goes, laid hands on each other, and not in the fashion of old buddies. We were not old buddies. In fact, I would have given a C-note to a sawbuck that as soon as they did spot me, if there were any way to manage it, any one of them or even all of them at once would take keen delight in killing hell out of me. However, there were a lot of other people around us, so I felt fairly safe — but only half safe, as those stinking ads say.

You wouldn't think a guy surrounded by forty or fifty thousand other people enjoying the races could pull off a killing and get away with it. Not in broad daylight. And not with a noisy gun. You wouldn't think so, maybe, but somebody had done just that. Two days ago, on Thursday afternoon, less than fifty yards from where I now sat, a man had been killed. Murdered. It had happened sometime around the end of the seventh race.

I didn't know who'd done the job — not for sure — but I was interested. I was *really* interested. Because the dead man had been a private detective. Like me. And he'd been working on a case at the time. Like me. The case, in fact, on which I was now working.

Doody wiggled a bit next to me, wrecking my thoughts, and said, "Black Velvet. Oh, that's a pretty name, such a *pretty* name."

She talked like that, sort of scattered, in a too-high voice with lots of blinking and wiggling. But, hell, you can't have everything. "Yeah," I said, "he's a so-so three-year-old. By Black Prince out of Velvet Dream," I added somewhat smugly.

She was impressed by my encyclopedic knowledge of horseflesh. And I was glad, since it wasn't exactly horseflesh I was interested in. I'll admit that, since I really was working, and since I figured at least two people had been killed already, one of them by me — not to mention the bullet brand on my fanny and the fresh lump on my skull — perhaps I should have been paying much less attention to Doody. But there is no point in concealing the widely known fact that tomatoes who look like Doody are my Achilles' heel, and that my Achilles' heel is the size of my foot.

So when Doody asked me would I please explain what that meant for little old her, I told her all about sires and dams and the naming of equine thoroughbreds.

"I see," she said brightly, "I see. And they usually sort of build the new horsie's name out of the mama and papa horsies' names?"

"Yeah, ugh," I said. "Yeah. That's how horsies — ahggh — how fillies and mares and geldings and such get their names. Not always, but often. This nag, though, hasn't got a prayer — "

"Then he could just as easily have been named, oh, Dream Prince, couldn't he? Dream Prince, out of those others, or what you said?"

"Well, I suppose so. Yeah, it could happen. But — "

"That settles it. That's my horsie. I'll bet on Dream Prince."

"Doody, for Pete's sake, that animal hasn't been in the money his last eighteen times out. He's a router running with older horses in a sprint. And Dream Prince isn't even his name — "

"Who cares?"

"Who *cares?* Don't you have any — "

"You're mad again."

She could tell when I was getting heated, I suppose, because I started scowling and glowering and raising my voice a bit, and shaking. Anyway, she looked up at me from those hot brown eyes and sort of squeezed them half shut, and wrinkled up her nose and wiggled her lips, and wiggled a bit elsewhere, and said, "I only want to bet on it because he reminds me of you, Shellie, See? Dream Prince? And you're — "

"Yeah. I remind you of a horse."

"You know what I intended to mean," she said.

"Yeah. Whatever that means." But the truth is, whether she intended to mean it or not, I was mollified. She could take the starch out of a man quicker than new Duz takes it out of an old shirt, even though all that wrinkling and wriggling was almost — not quite, but almost — nauseating. And of course she was built — well, you wouldn't believe it.

"So O.K.," I said. "Bet on the nag."

"You buy me a ticket, Shellie."

I bought her a two-dollar win ticket on whatever its name was — Prince Blackness or something. Then I bought a twenty-dollar win ticket on the solid horse in the race, Red Acorn.

I got back to our seats just as the bell rang and the track announcer cried, "Theeere they go!" and the horses sprang from the starting gate. Then, very soon, the announcer was crying, ". . . and it's Black Velvet by three lengths, Red Acorn and Easy Time . . ."

Doody was squealing and making happy noises next to me, then she stopped and looked at me. "You're mad again, aren't you?"

"Mad?" I said. "Me, mad? Are you nuts? Are you out of your stupid mind? Why would I be mad?"

"Well, you're all red in the face, and making fists out of your fists, and look like you're going to die or something."

It was ridiculous. I merely happen to have an encyclopedic knowledge of horseflesh. And had already doped the first few races utilizing the *Daily Racing Form* and a very scientific system I'd worked out, with emphasis on days since the last race, class, lengths gained or lost in the stretch, whether the horse finished in the money, and such vital factors as those.

And ". . . Black Velvet by three lengths . . ."

"But, Shellie," she said, "we won, didn't we?"

"No. You won."

"You didn't?"

"How could — No. Simply, it is impossible for both of us to win, since we bet on different horses."

"You're mad."

"No. No. No."

"Just because I didn't go into a fit or something with numbers and things and picked his pretty name instead. What's wrong with that?"

"Nothing. It's just not . . . very scientific."

"Oh, scientific, pooh," she said. Then, softly, "Shellie, I'm sorry you lost. Really." She was taking the press out of my pants again.

"My horse came in second," I said.

"Well, that's better than nowhere, isn't it?"

"I'm not sure. I'm not even sure I know what that means."

She was looking at my ticket, all crumpled and sweaty, then at her own ticket. "Why did you spend twenty dollars on the one who was second, and only two dollars on my horsie?"

I said deliberately, "If you . . . don't quit calling . . . those animals 'horsies' I will — "

"Don't you yell at me!"

I closed my eyes, beat my clenched fists lightly on my head, and said nothing. Just once, I thought, I'd like to be a woman. I'd probably kill myself, but I would sure like to know what it's like.

"Dear," I said. "Dear Doody. Really, I've got work to do. Pretend I'm on the track of a gang of desperate criminals — which I really am, incredible as that may seem in the midst of all this gaiety — and that I must concentrate my undivided attention on clues and — "

"How much did I win?" she asked me.

I was afraid to look at the tote board. I looked. Black Velvet, at thirty-three to one, had paid sixty-eight dollars. "You won," I said in a voice like Death's rattle, "sixty-six dollars. Sixty-eight, counting my two bucks."

I'll give Doody this: she didn't make any further comment. She was already looking at the horses entered in the second race.

By the time the sixth race ended, nothing very important had happened. Nothing very good, that is. I'd kept looking for the man I expected to see here, but he hadn't shown up. Scalzo and his two buddy boys still hadn't spotted me, apparently.

The only noteworthy thing was that Doody, by the end of the sixth race, had won three hundred and eighty dollars. And I had lost three hundred and ninety dollars. It was almost perfect, I thought. It would have been perfect if I'd fallen down and broken a leg. And if I'd broken a leg, probably somebody would have come along and shot me. And if somebody had shot me, Doody would have won a bet on it.

Ah, but Doody was gay. Alive. Bright and bubbling. She sickened me. Horsies sickened me. Life sickened me.

Doody eyed me intently, her beautiful dopey face showing concern. "Ah, hon," she said, "you're just tired. Let me take you home, and fix you some food or a drink or some coffee, and put you to bed."

"The hell," I said, "with the food and the drink and the coffee." Wasn't it ever thus? The miserable truth, however, was that I couldn't leave the track. Not yet, anyway. I knew something was going to happen this day. Maybe not here at the track, but if not here, then very damned soon after the last race. Because, if nothing else, I was going to make it happen.

The track announcer's voice came over the public-address system, telling us of weight and equipment changes in the upcoming mile-and-a-sixteenth route, an allowance race. The bugler tooted his trumpet, the horses came onto the track. I'd lost six races in a row; maybe I'd have better luck with this one, the seventh.

The seventh — that was the race when my predecessor on this case had been killed, I realized. The seventh, on Thursday. It gave me a kind of creepy prickliness along my spine. But that's ridiculous, I thought. Ha-ha, I thought. That's being superstitious, and I'm not superstitious, I thought, crossing my fingers and looking for wood to knock on, and not finding any wood. Just in case, by some freak of circumstance, I *did* get killed, I hoped my horse won the race; I would hate to die a loser.

Something else bothered me. The man I'd expected to see here still hadn't shown up. Maybe I was wrong. And maybe Doody had been lying to me. I looked at her, wondering about her still, and thinking of how much had happened since we'd met, less than twenty-four hours ago.

Her name was really Nell Duden, she'd said, and she told me she loathed the name Nell. I'd thought that was pretty smart of her. That's how it started — with me thinking she was smart.

Actually, the ball had started rolling a few hours before I met Doody. Started Friday afternoon with a phone call from big, lusty Gabriel Rothstein, financial wizard, multi-zillionaire. . . .

Two

I'd hit my downtown L.A. office Friday afternoon just after 1 P.M. I clattered up a flight of stairs in the Hamilton Building, waved a hello to Hazel, the cute little gal at the switchboard, unlocked the door lettered SHELDON SCOTT, INVESTIGATIONS, and went inside.

After opening a window and looking down at the citizens on Broadway, then up at the gathering smog while inhaling a few lungfuls of it through a long cigarette, equipped with a filter to remove some of the gasoline, I walked over to the bookcase and fed the fish. Busy, busy, the mad life of a private eye.

The fish are guppies, splendidly colorful and singularly amorous little creatures, which I have trapped in a ten-gallon tank atop the office bookcase. I sprinkled a bit of powdered salmon meal on the water's surface and movement in the tank became more frenzied, drab females and brightly colored males leaving their sport momentarily to gobble a small hunk of nourishment. Then with hunger pangs — or whatever pangs fish feel — temporarily assuaged, they returned to the attack, to the assuagement of other pangs.

The one gravid female, which last night had been heavy with young, I now noted was thin again. She'd given birth to a litter during the night, obviously; but none of the young were now in sight. You've got to keep a sharp eye on them, the sweet little things; they eat their babies.

Well, with all that accomplished, there wasn't a damn thing left to do. I'd wrapped up a peculiar insurance fraud three days ago — the culprit had returned the gross of glass eyes he'd stolen — and since then life had been a wild whirl of nothing.

I reached for the phone, thinking it wouldn't hurt a bit to call Carmen and try making a date for a late lunch or early dinner. Carmen was a hot five-foot, eight-inch tamale who performed a cha-cha like a Mexican revolution, and I figured we might have a belt or two and then a few tacos or something, like out in some isolated picnic grounds or sand dunes. Understand, I rarely drink when I'm working — though sometimes I'll knock off work for an hour or two — but since there was no fascinating case on the agenda, perhaps I could stir up a Mexican revolution.

I had my hand on the phone when it rang. Maybe it was a good omen, I thought. Maybe it was Carmen, calling me for a change. O.K., I'd give her a change. It wasn't Carmen.

The voice charged out of the earpiece like Teddy Roosevelt taking San Juan Hill, like a verbal avalanche, like the bull eating up the *torero*.

"Hello. Mr. Scott? Mr. Sheldon Scott?"

"Ow," I said. "Hey, wait till I put the phone on my other ear." I stuck a finger in my right ear and waggled it around. "Yeah, this is Shell Scott. You want to hire a half-deaf detective?"

"Sorry. Sorry," be boomed. Then he got his rumbling voice down a few decibels. "When there's something urgent on my mind I'm inclined to speak with unnecessary emphasis."

"You're kidding."

"If you're not critically busy at the moment I'd like to employ you on an undertaking of the greatest importance. I am Gabriel Rothstein."

"Fine, undertakings are part of my business. And at the moment I'm not critically busy. I've already fed the fish."

"What's that?"

"Never mind. What — " I stopped, the name Gabriel Rothstein stirring half-hidden memory. It was a name easy enough to remember, but I hadn't heard or seen it more than a few times. I glance at the financial pages only occasionally, and then usually when I'm hunting for the sports section, but that's where I'd seen the name. He was some kind of financial genius or Wall Street wonder, and I'd noted items about his waging a proxy fight or being elected to a board of directors a time or two. I couldn't figure why a man who could buy buildings like I buy bullets would be interested in hiring me. So I asked him.

Richard S. Prather

"I'd prefer not to discuss this on the phone, Mr. Scott. If you'll come immediately to my office — top floor of the Rothstein Building on Fifth Street — I'll explain in detail."

Immediately, he'd said. And there was a kind of no-nonsense urgency about this guy — his voice, anyway — that seemed to snap, "Action! Action!" So I said, "Open the door. Goodbye."

"Good-bye."

We hung up.

I went out of the office, waved to Hazel, and trotted down to Broadway, past Pete's — a bar in which owner-bartender Pete has cured, and caused, many of my hangovers — to the adjacent parking lot, and into my new Cadillac convertible. Sky-blue, with white-leather upholstery and a copy of Omar Khayyám. Ah, Carmen, I fear we'll not Khayyám in the dunes today.

My office is on Broadway between Third and Fourth, so it was only four blocks to the Rothstein Building. The lights and traffic were with me and I found a parking slot twenty feet from the building's double doors and trotted through them just in time to catch the elevator going up.

It was an elevator with a uniformed attendant, and when I said quietly, "Twelve," he stiffened to attention and we zipped straight to the top, while four other passengers headed for less lofty levels scowled at me. It made me a bit uncomfortable, but hell, Rothstein owned the building, didn't he?

Hiss of air as the doors opened then closed behind me, polished hallway left and right, and straight ahead a wooden door with small black letters: G. ROTHSTEIN.

I knocked and the door rattled as a man's voice from inside — it could only have been Gabriel Rothstein's — thundered, "Come in."

In I went. It was a big room, gray carpet, dark-paneled walls, low ceiling. Along the walls were tables with stacks of papers and magazines on them. Straight ahead of me, before an enormous window which looked down on Fifth Street, was a large black desk behind which sat a man. He stood up, and seemed to keep on standing up for quite awhile.

"Excellent," he boomed at me. "Excellent, Mr. Scott. You are not a man who dawdles."

"I hurried," I said. "Just in case you've got money."

10

It could have been the wrong note, if it turned out G. Rothstein was one of those stuffy billionaires — which was one of the things I wanted to know about him. But he threw back his head and laughter boomed up from his thick middle and through his even thicker chest past a corded neck, and filled the room with happy thunder.

"Sometimes I scuttle a yacht," he said, "just to get a girl in a thin dress wet."

This time I laughed, and he asked me what I'd meant about having already fed the fish, and I told him, and for a minute or two we just tossed the conversational ball around.

Then he said, "Well, you're hired, Mr. Scott. The only question remaining is whether you care to take the job." He paused. "If it's of interest to you, this isn't a snap decision. I've had you investigated since yesterday afternoon." He paused again. "And when I have a man investigated I learn a great deal about him."

"I'll be damned," I said, with real surprise. I've had characters checking up on me before, but so far as I knew this was the first time I'd had not even an inkling that it was being done. My business is investigation, and the asset above all others of any investigator is his sources of information, his informers and tipsters and informants. I think my sources are second to none in Los Angeles, but I'd not heard a rumble, not a peep. Not yet, anyway; probably later today I'd get the word, but none had reached me yet. Consequently my opinion of Gabriel Rothstein — already high enough on first impression — went up a notch.

"I'll be damned," I said again. Then I added, "But I'll bet you don't know about Carmen."

He grinned, a big white-toothed tigerish grin, and said nothing. The sonofabitch! He *did* know about Carmen.

Here in the spacious room his voice was bearable, even pleasant. Actually, it wasn't that he yelled or shouted, simply that he had a crackling, magnetic voice that, even when throttled down, sounded like a soft train wreck. He was a powerful man, big, burly, with energy leaking out of him. A big man, a bull of a man, but nonetheless a damned good-looking man. Not good-looking in the classic or magazine-cover sense, but the kind of virile rugged male who a century or two ago might have scouted trails west through the forests, biting bears in the neck and scalping Indians.

He was, I'd guess, about six feet, four inches tall, a couple of inches over my six-two, and if he weighed fifty pounds he weighed at least two-fifty. His hair was cut even shorter than mine, black, and his skin was dark, smooth-shaven, and deeply tanned. Straight black brows hung low and level over dark, almost cold, blue eyes. A big beak of a nose speared down toward a wide mouth, and when he smiled, white teeth flashed against the darkness of his skin.

We were seated at opposite sides of his large black desk now. Around the room, on the tables I'd noticed earlier, were stacks of *The Wall Street Journal, Barron's, Forbes*, bound volumes of *The Value Line Investment Survey*, and other publications I'd never heard of. On the desk before him were an open copy of the newspaper-size *Wall Street Journal* and a magazine with "Electronics" in its title.

"Tools of the trade," Rothstein said, noting my glance around the room. "My business is investment. Or speculation, if you prefer. I make — and sometimes lose — money in the market. More precisely, by becoming a part owner of companies which my investigation leads me to believe will grow at a faster rate than the economy, the market, and other similar companies within the industry. I own all the blue chips I want or need — IBM, Du Pont, General Motors, and the like — and I now concentrate exclusively on the larger risk with consequent larger potential for gain."

"Playing the long shots, in other words."

"Yes, in a way." He ran a finger down the bridge of his nose. "Are you familiar with the stock market, Mr. Scott?"

I shook my head. "Look, Mr. Rothstein, let it be said immediately that, while I am very familiar with the m.o. of Hymie the Rat, who burgles with a flair and is fruit for cheese, when it comes to the price of U.S. Lead or the shenanigans of corporation presidents — "

"You'll be meeting a corporation president this afternoon, Mr. Scott."

"But — "

"I know what I'm doing." He cut me off with the wave of a beefy hand. "It would be quicker if I disposed of your objections before you raise them."

I shrugged. Yeah. If he could do it. So, O.K., I'd listen.

He went on, "More than a year ago I became interested in the possibilities of a company, Universal Electronics, which has been listed on

12

the American Exchange since nineteen sixty-one. Very interested. Excited, even. It was the most promising speculation I had uncovered in two years. Primarily because the director of research and development of UE — Universal Electronics — was a man, a man of genius I shall say, named Ryder Tangier."

"Tangier. Didn't I read — "

The wave of his hand again, with a smile. "The stock was then grossly underpriced. I bought forty thousand shares at an average of eight, and instituted a more intensive investigation of the company, its management, products, history, potential. I became convinced that when research then being conducted — in ultrasonics, bionics, lasers, cryogenics, microminiaturization — eventuated in consumer products already in various stages of development, the stock would rise to twenty, thirty — actually there was almost no reasonable limit. A half million invested in UE could become several millions within a year or two, a capital gain, taxable at only twenty-five per cent instead of ninety-one per cent. An exciting prospect, is it not?"

"I hope to shout."

"My investigations, and personal discussions with officials of the company, including Mr. Tangier, convinced me that the company's — primarily Mr. Tangier's — greatest inventions, discoveries, new products lay ahead, in the near future. I bought forty-five thousand more shares, at an average of nine. A few days later the bottom dropped out. Auditors uncovered a shortage — only seventy-six thousand dollars, a relatively small amount, but a shortage — and evidence clearly pointed to Ryder Tangier as the thief. He has since been tried, and a month ago was sent to prison." He paused. "I assume, from your initial reaction to the name, that you're familiar with the case?"

"The name at least. I remember reading something about the trial. Not much."

"There wasn't much in the general news. Primarily the story was stressed in financial journals. Well, the stock dropped from a high of ten and three-eighths to seven, then to five. It is now three and five-eighths. I had no stop-loss on my UE stock — in fact, when the story broke I was on my yacht, en route to Acapulco and deliberately taking a sabbatical from the financial news — so I was not stopped out. Consequently, I now own eighty-five thousand shares of UE for which I paid, exclusive of fees and commissions, seven hundred and twenty-five thousand dollars. Worse, the anticipated rise, which might easily have netted me a million capital gain, or more, has evaporated." He stopped, grinned again, and said, "I assume this is painful to you, Mr. Scott."

"I am bleeding profusely, Mr. Rothstein. And my brilliant logic tells me that, somehow, you hope still to make that million or so. But how I enter into this delicious coup, I fail — "

"I come to that now. Mr. Tangier went to prison protesting his innocence — "

"Which is s.o.p. For those who plead not guilty, anyhow."

"Which he did. More, he contended that his fellow board member-old friend and cofounder of Universal Electronics — one Matthew Wyndham, must in fact be guilty of the embezzlement, since he had induced him to sign papers, write checks, open dummy accounts and had so arranged the evidence that it would point to Ryder Tangier. Mr. Matthew Wyndham is president of Universal Electronics. He is the corporation president whom, as I indicated a few minutes ago, you will meet today."

"If I take the case."

"I think you will, Mr. Scott. What I want you to do is determine to your own satisfaction whether Ryder Tangier is in truth guilty of the embezzlement. Should you decide he is not guilty, then obviously someone else is. In that case I want you to discover the identity of that person, whether it is the president, Matthew Wyndham, or any other member of the board or person intimately associated with the company. I want you to assume an overwhelming interest in learning the truth, as if you yourself were an owner of the company, and take any action or risk required — with caution, of course. Without a sense of undue urgency." He paused. "And I believe I know enough about you now, Mr. Scott, to know that when I have completed my explanation you will be dying to take the case."

"I'm not crazy about the way you said that."

"Eager to take the case, then."

"I'll go along with eager." I did go along with eager; the guy had me interested now — not hooked, but interested.

Then he hooked me. Twice.

"We come now," he said, "to Axel Scalzo."

I sat up straighter. "Scalzo? That sonofabitch? What's he got to do with this?"

"Possibly nothing, perhaps a good deal. He owns a large block of Universal Electronics stock. More, he was buying that stock even before I made my initial investment in the company — and has continued to purchase shares, several thousand in the last few weeks, *since* the scandal, since the shares dropped to their all-time low. It may be that he knows something that even I do not know. If so, it would be greatly to my advantage to know what it is."

"Yeah. Especially when the man is Scalzo."

"You do know who he is, then?"

I nodded. I knew the s.o.b. We had never gotten intimate, like shooting each other, but one of my first cases in this town, a few months after I'd opened the office, had been a simple extortion case. A businessman, a friend of mine, was being shaken down by two unhealthy-looking characters, whom I braced and told off, and who later got in the first lick at me with a sap, then proceeded to bash me about the head and kick in two of my ribs. Still later, I caught them one at a time and put them both in the hospital, and one of them now walked with a permanent limp.

The point of the story is that after the whole thing simmered down, the extortion attempt kaput, I learned the two men had been working for Axel Scalzo. No proof; just the word from one of my informants, an ex-con named Sick Eddy Sly. I had good reason to believe that since then more than one of the mugs I'd beefed with, or even sent away to the graveyard, had been associated, one way or another, with Scalzo. But it had never come to a head; it just floated in the bad blood between us like a boil about to settle down and hatch.

"Yeah," I said. "I know Scalzo."

"Would you say he is a gangster? A racketeer?"

"A hoodlum — and I'd say so. If you asked me to prove it, I couldn't, not in court. Not at the moment, anyway. But take my word for it, he is."

"It disturbs me that so unsavory an individual seems to be taking such an interest in Universal Electronics."

"It would disturb me too, if I owned eighty-five thousand shares of the stock. Though I suppose he's got as much right to buy shares in the company as anybody else. Not much harm in that, is there?"

"There might well be great harm — and take my word for *that*, Mr. Scott. Each share of common stock is not only evidence of ownership and equity in the company which issued it, but also a vote. Owners of common stock elect the directors of the company, and those directors elect the officers who run the company. In other words, the common-stockholders determine the management — to me the most important factor in any company — by the election of directors who determine the policy. I'll not burden you with details of all the ramifications of potential disaster — to thousands, even millions, of stockholders — when men of less than complete integrity become able to influence or even control the policy and expenditures of a corporation."

He scowled, looking past me. "But I would refer you to Frank Coster, born Phillip Musica, who stole uncounted millions from McKesson & Robbins in the late twenties and the thirties and who, when exposed, blew out his brains — which was little consolation to McKesson & Robbins stockholders. To brilliant Lowell McAfee Birrell, who fled to Brazil and is now facing numerous indictments, only one of them being the matter of manipulation of Swan-Finch and Doeskin stock, through which manipulation stockholders were fraudulently relieved of approximately fourteen million dollars. To the complex machinations of Alexander Guterma, who in the mid-fifties acquired control of three companies listed on the New York Stock Exchange, engaged in massive swindling — and again, though he was convicted of fraud and sentenced to prison, this was little consolation to those defrauded. And finally to the increasing efforts of gangsters and rack-eteers to control legitimate businesses through the stock market, by investing their criminal profits in securities of those businesses. As in the case of Stanley Younger, who was associated with convicted felons Lombardozzi, Tortorello, and DeFilippo in boiler-room promotion and manipulation of watered stock — Atlas Gypsum, Shoreland Mines, National Photocopy, Monarch Asbestos . . . ." Rothstein was silent for a few seconds, then smiled. "Of course, Mr. Scalzo may merely be investing some of his capital, putting his money to work for him in a promising corporation. On the other hand . . ."

"I get a glimmer of light."

"My final major illumination, then. One which, before you accept or decline my offer of employment, you should know. A week ago — to do the job which I am now asking you to do — I employed another detective. He learned little, but enough to reinforce my conviction that Ryder Tangier is indeed innocent of the crime for which he is now serving a prison sentence." He paused. "You can appreciate that if Mr. Tangier *is* innocent, and can be cleared, and return to Universal Electronics — which I know to be his desire — the future again will be golden. On the other hand, without Ryder Tangier, UE is merely another electronics corporation."

"Sure. *If* he's innocent, the bowl is still full of gravy. The bit I don't understand is why, if you've got one investigator working on this for you, you want to hire another."

"You will be the only investigator working on it, Mr. Scott. The first one, unfortunately, is dead. He was killed yesterday, at Hollywood Park, during one of the races."

He stopped. And I could feel it starting. The queer tickle in my stomach, the gentle tightening of my spine. "I don't suppose," I said, "that he was kicked by a horse."

"No. He was shot in the back."

Three

I stubbed out another cigarette.

Gabriel Rothstein's comment about Hollywood Park told me the murdered detective was a man named John Kay. I'd learned of his death yesterday. I'd known Kay, not well, but we'd met a time or two, had a few drinks together. He had been an old-timer, with a lot of experience, intelligent and capable. But not intelligent and capable enough — or lucky enough — to stay alive this time.

Rothstein had no idea why John Kay had been murdered. Possibly it was because of the case on which he had been — and, I guessed, I now was — working. But his death could very well have been due to circumstances completely unconnected with his job for Rothstein. It might have been due to his checking on Tangier and Universal Electronics, or Matthew Wyndham, or Axel Scalzo, or the stock market — or missing Aunt Suzie, heir to dad's wig factory. He'd just been shot, period; that was all anybody, including the police, knew.

I said, "You figure Tangier was stuck with a frame, right? Is that what Kay came up with?"

"In part. Shortly after Mr. Tangier was arrested, I met and talked with him myself, and was greatly impressed by the man, his brilliance and apparent integrity. As for Mr. Kay, on Wednesday night, the night before he was killed, he reported to me by phone and stated that he shared my opinion as to Mr. Tangier's innocence, though he as yet had no concrete evidence to support that belief. However, he said he had talked earlier that night to Mr. Tangier's daughter and believed that, acting on information she had given him, he might have more concrete evidence in a day or two."

"Tangier's daughter?"

"Yes, Julie Tangier. A young girl whose brilliance equals her father's, I would say. And beautiful as well, a striking red-haired creature with all the feminine endowments, in addition to a remarkably keen brain."

"What did she tell him?"

"Mr. Kay did not specify."

"Well, if she told Kay, maybe she'd tell me. Where is she now?"

"I presume she is still at the Watson-Parker Hotel on Wilshire Boulevard. That is where I talked to her."

"When was this?"

"Approximately a month ago, slightly more, perhaps. When Mr. Tangier was arrested, his daughter was out of the country, in Europe I believe. Apparently she didn't learn of her father's difficulty until long after he'd been arrested, and then she flew straight to Los Angeles. Subsequent to my last interview with Mr. Tangier I went to the Watson-Parker, where he told me she was staying, and talked to her. She, of course, had no evidence that could help her father, and merely insisted he couldn't possibly be guilty. I was greatly impressed by both of them." Rothstein fell silent, running an index finger down the bridge of his nose.

I said, "You say Kay had come around to thinking Tangier was innocent. Had he tagged anybody he thought *was* guilty?"

"No, at least he did not so report to me. We know, of course, that Mr. Tangier thought his friend, Mr. Wyndham, was the responsible person. That's a strange thing, however."

"How?"

"Mr. Wyndham is a millionaire. Why would he embezzle a paltry seventy-six thousand dollars?"

"Why indeed? But wouldn't the same reasoning apply to Tangier?"

"To some extent, yes. His net worth is approximately two hundred thousand dollars exclusive of — I repeat, exclusive of — his sixty thousand shares of stock in the company. Mr. Wyndham's wife is herself quite wealthy, and Matthew Wyndham, when the firm was incorporated nearly ten years ago, provided nearly all of the original capital. Mr. Tangier's contribution was, essentially, his brain. Which, I assure you, could be worth many millions of dollars to Universal Electronics. And possibly to me." He plucked at the point of his nose. "I have no answers, Mr. Scott. I merely give you what facts are in my possession. I want you to provide the answers." He looked at me and smiled. "Will you?"

"I'll give it a good try." I thought a minute. "About Axel Scalzo, Mr. Rothstein. I've never heard of his being interested in stocks or the market. So naturally I'm curious that his name would crop up here. Do you know of any connection between him and Ryder Tangier?"

"No."

"How about the president of the company, this Matthew Wyndham?"

Rothstein shook his head. "No, I have been unable to uncover any evidence that Mr. Scalzo even knows of the existence of Mr. Tangier or Mr. Wyndham — or anyone else associated with UE. On the surface, at least, Mr. Scalzo is simply a man who has purchased a sizable amount of Universal Electronics stock. I suspect others may also be buying UE stock for him, so it won't appear in his name, but stock that he could vote."

"How's that?"

"The annual stockholders' meeting of the company is scheduled for Monday. Three days from now. There is this . . . index of urgency, I might say. But I don't wish this to unnecessarily accelerate your investigation, or lead you to take unnecessary risks. At Monday's stockholders' meeting the new board of directors will be elected. Or reelected. Should Mr. Scalzo control, directly or indirectly, a sufficient number of shares, he might be able to elect a director or two." He sighed. "However, I don't intend for you to worry about that, Mr. Scott. I certainly don't expect you to accomplish all I ask by Monday."

I grunted. "Kay knocked off yesterday. Stockholders' meeting this coming Monday. You're hiring me today — "

"Yes," he interrupted, nodding. "Events do seem to be moving toward a focus, don't they?"

"Or a boil," I said.

In the next few minutes Rothstein covered some incidental points and gave me his card, which bore only his name and two phone numbers. He explained that he was seldom in his office after 3 or 4 P.M., and the card listed the number for his office and also his home in the San Fernando Valley. I stuck the card in my wallet and was ready to go.

Almost ready. When we discussed my fee, Rothstein smiled oddly, reached into his coat pocket, and pulled out a folded piece of paper.

Holding it in two fingers he said, "I have been informed that your usual fee, for an investigation of this nature is a hundred dollars a day."

"Plus unusual expenses. Right."

He handed me the paper. "This is what I intend to pay you, Mr. Scott. This and only this. Whether your investigation requires a day — or a year — of your time. And you must give me your solemn word that you will complete the investigation, without fanfare, especially without involving me, if possible."

This guy kept hooking me. With real interest, I unfolded the heavy rectangle of intricately engraved paper and saw the figures "1000" in the upper corners. "This," I said, "is the damndest thousand-dollar bill I ever saw."

"It is much more than that, Mr. Scott. Or much less. I have signed the certificate on its back and — while eventually it will have to be sent to the company's transfer agent and be reissued — it is now in your name. You own one thousand shares of common stock in Universal Electronics, Incorporated. You are now a part owner of the company."

I started getting it.

He went on, "At this moment the stock certificate in your hand is worth approximately three thousand, six hundred and twenty-five dollars. If your investigation requires a month, you will receive slightly better than one hundred dollars a day. But if you should complete the job in a week . . ."

He smiled.

I smiled. "And if I should operate like a madman and not get killed and free all the slaves and wrap this up in the next forty minutes . . ."

"Precisely." He was enjoying himself. "You would be earning whatever you're really worth."

He waited. Waited as if expecting me to say something else. And for about three seconds I had no idea what it could be — and then it smacked me all at once, like simultaneous hot and cold showers. "Hey, this goddamn thing could be worth — hell, approximately twenty bucks if — "

"Precisely," he said again, playing happily with his beak. "Should Mr. Tangier in fact be guilty, or should you fail to prove his innocence, or for any other combination of reasons should the company founder or fail, it is quite possible that the stock will soon be worth even less than it is today. It might eventually reach a value of — nothing."

I glowered at him. "Great That's all I need. Nothing. And a hole in my head for laughs. Great — "

"On the other hand, consider this. If all that I hope comes to pass, and if the future of Universal Electronics is as bright as I visualize it, the stock might in time climb to twenty, forty, it could even split, climb to forty again. . . . It is entirely possible that your thousand UE shares will eventually be worth, oh, let's say fifty thousand dollars."

Wow, I thought. Fifty G's. Not bad for a couple days' work. Money floated before my eyes. Visions of sugarplums danced in my head. In all three primary colors. Blonde, brunette, and redhead.

"We have an agreement, Mr. Scott?" he asked.

"We do. And you are a monster, Mr. Rothstein. You do not want me needled by any sense of urgency. Not *much*, you don't."

He laughed, thunderously.

I looked at the stock certificate in my hand, getting a whole new feeling about this case. What I did in the next few days, or even hours, might very well have a great deal to do with what that hunk of paper would eventually be worth. It slowly sank into my noodle: I was indeed a part owner of Universal Electronics. I was now vitally interested in whether its products were good or bad, whether it succeeded or failed, in the management of the company, Matthew Wyndham among others, and of course Ryder Tangier — and I hadn't met a damned one of them yet. And if Scalzo was, in some complicated fashion, trying to muscle in on UE, why, the s.o.b. was trying to muscle into *my* company.

I looked at Rothstein and said slowly, "You know, you're pretty good."

He smiled.

I grinned at him and said, "Well, we've got a deal. And I like it this way."

He grinned back. "I thought you would."

He walked with me to the door. With the door open, I paused for a last word.

"I just thought of something else," I said. "I know there's all the time in the world. No hurry, nothing like that. And I shouldn't stick my neck out, of course. But I'll bet it wouldn't actually displease you if somehow, even if I got killed doing it, I managed to tie everything up in a ribbon before Monday. Before that annual stockholders' meeting."

"It is gratifying, Mr. Scott," he said, "that you do in time become aware of the obvious."

We grinned at each other again, and I left.

Four

For a while I just sat in the Cad, smoking a cigarette and lining up what Rothstein had told me.

There were four separate hunks to chew on, it seemed to me. First and of prime importance was the embezzlement, the theft from Universal Electronics and the guilt or innocence of UE's brainy backbone, Ryder Tangier. Next was the question — just in case Tangier was innocent — of the guilty party's identity, whether that party was Matthew Wyndham or somebody else intimately associated with UE. Then there was Axel Scalzo, and what skulduggery — if any — he might be up to. And, finally, the murder of John Kay.

There might be no connection at all among those chunks; or there might be among them two or more pieces of the same puzzle. If puzzle there was.

If Ryder Tangier had in truth swiped the loot and legitimately gone to the sneezer, then that was it, period. No point in checking on Wyndham or anybody else at UE. Scalzo was just playing the market. Kay had been knocked off by Aunt Suzie. But if he hadn't . . . I got busy.

From the police I learned that John Kay had been shot in the back with a .38, the gun held against his coat and the bullet severing his spine. It had happened during or after the running of the seventh race, on the ground level in front of the grandstand, near the rail, only a few yards from the gate leading into — or out from — the Clubhouse. That area, almost directly opposite the finish line, is generally the most crowded spot at the track, especially during and at the end of a race. There must have been thousands of people milling around when it happened, but nobody had been found who'd heard a shot or noticed anything unusual.

The police had located a man named Murphy, with whom Kay had keen sitting, but he said he'd never met Kay until that day. Kay had asked if he could share Murphy's box, and Murphy, alone and glad to have company, had agreed. He'd gone to place a bet on the seventh race and when he returned to his box Kay was gone. He didn't see him again, and hadn't even known Kay was dead until the police questioned him. Murphy was a solid citizen, married, respectable, and the police didn't doubt his story. There were no leads, no clues, just a bullet in Kay's back.

As far as the police and the D.A.'s office were concerned, Ryder Tangier had been guilty as hell and the verdict a just one. He'd had no defense except denial, and the police had no real reason to suspect Matthew Wyndham or anybody else in the company.

I got a transcript of the trial, but merely thumbed through it; there was no time to read it then, and the D.A.'s office had given me the salient facts, anyway. Among the meager testimony given in Ryder Tangier's behalf, had been, perhaps surprisingly, testimony from Matthew Wyndham's personal secretary, a Miss Alice Brandt. Her appearance had been as a character witness, and her personal opinion about what "a nice, honest man" Tangier was clearly hadn't impressed the jury. Despite the fact that — according to police friends of mine — she was a "damned good-looking blonde," built like a brick brick-factory.

John Kay had been head of a six-man agency, "O.K. Investigators," but the other members of his staff couldn't help me; they didn't know what he'd done on the day of, or the day previous to, his murder. And they didn't have the faintest idea why he'd been at the race track. Kay had been unmarried, lived alone; no help there.

I hired one of the big L.A. agencies to do a fast check on all of the Universal Electronics directors and key personnel, routine that would take too much time for me to handle alone. Matthew Wyndham I meant to check out myself. Then I drove to the Watson-Parker.

It was a big white hotel on Wilshire, plush and expensive, its dining room one of the most popular spots in town among those who didn't mind paying four dollars for a hamburger. At the desk I asked for Julie Tangier.

The desk clerk, a short, pleasant-faced man, seemed a bit uneasy as he said, "Miss Tangier is not in, sir."

"Oh?" In a big hotel, the desk clerks rarely know all the guests, and whether they're in or out of their rooms — at least not without checking first. But the answer had been on the tip of his tongue. I said, "Well, what's her room number? I'll call or come back later."

He glanced past me and nodded.

In a moment a second man joined us. "Hello, Scott. What you want?" Then to the desk clerk, "It's O.K., I know him."

The second man was a middle-aged red-faced guy, a former policeman named McCoy, now "public relations coordinator" for the Watson-Parker. In other words, the house detective.

"Hi, McCoy," I said. "What's the mystery? I merely asked to see Julie Tangier."

He shrugged. "First of this month she pays a month in advance on her suite — five hundred and fifty bucks. She was around a day or two, I'm not sure how long, then she's just not around any more."

"She checked out?"

"No, she didn't check out. Like I said, she's just not around any more. What'd you want with her, Scott?"

"Just a talk. What the hell? She take her stuff? You know, clothes and — "

"Not a thing, far as I can tell. Clothes, bags, makeup, like lipsticks and all, they're still in the rooms. Everything's there but Miss Tangier."

"O.K. if I take a look?"

"Sure. Come on."

He went with me up to a corner suite. I looked around, but it didn't do me any good. There were a lot of expensive clothes, ten pairs of high-heeled shoes, the usual feminine things, including makeup. Everything but Julie.

When I left, I asked McCoy to let me know if she showed, thanked him, and said next time I was by I'd bring along a jug of bourbon.

"Make it Johnny Walker Red," he said. "I'm drinking Scotch these nights."

I told him it was a deal and went out.

I'd phoned half a dozen of my "underworld" informants earlier in the day, and now I was looking for Sick Eddy Sly. He'd fallen twice for burglary, once from Sacramento and once from L.A., and done two jolts in San Quentin. Since the last bit he'd been out for four years, always "on the verge of imminent dyin'" to hear him tell it.

Eddy knew practically every thief, grifter, and heavy man in Southern California, and was one of the most valuable sources of info I had. A year ago I'd been hired by a man whose home safe had been torched and emptied of forty thousand clams in cash. I turned up the thief without leaving my office by phoning Eddy Sly and asking him if he knew who'd pulled the heist. The police picked the thief up with the loot, and I gave Eddy my five-hundred-buck fee, more as an investment in the future than as payment for service rendered. As a result, Eddy was always anxious to tell me more.

I found him in his room at the Gable Hotel. Still sleeping, at four in the afternoon. He let me in when I knocked, mumbled something unintelligible, then plodded barefoot back over the carpet to his mussed bed and slumped down on it. He was wearing shorts and a cotton undershirt with a hole in it, and did not look like Charles Atlas.

He was called Sick Eddy because about three-fourths of his conversation was devoted to descriptions of his real or imaginary ailments. He was a hypochondriac's hypochondriac, but he sure didn't look well. His complexion was the shade of sick oysters, his eyes were perpetually bloodshot, and he was so skinny he must have had a thin skeleton. All in all, he looked like Dracula in daylight. He was forty-eight years old, about five-six, with sparse black hair streaked with gray on his narrow head, and a brown mole on his long upper lip.

"Oo-oh," he groaned. "Waowoo." He shook his head, smacked his lips. "Think I got athaletes' foot in my mouth." He got up and thumped to a washbasin visible through the open bathroom door. He took a slug from a bottle of Old Crow, gargled noisily, swallowed with the sound of water going down a bathtub drain, then came back and sat on the bed again.

"That killed the little athaletes," he said morosely. Silence.

"Sheldon," he said finally, aiming the red eyes at me, "the private fuzz. What the hell. What brings you calling on this fine day? Or night. What is it?"

"Four P.M. How you feeling, Eddy?" It was a question I had to ask him. He'd never forgive me if I didn't ask.

He smiled slightly, cherishing his agony. "What kind of question is that?" he said. "Same as usual — worse than usual." He peered around the room. "Where you at?"

I found his bifocals on a bedside table and handed them to him. He put them on, saying, "Don't make no difference. My eyes is so bad I can't see my glasses." He burped, lovingly. "Man, I got more gas than Standard Oil. What you want, Scott?"

"I guess you heard about John Kay getting hit yesterday."

Eddy nodded. "Yeah, he got pooped at Hollypark, didn't he?"

"Right. Any rumbles about it?"

"None reached me. You're curious about who knocked him down, huh?"

"And how."

"Well, there ain't been nothin' on the wire about it, Scott. But I'll get on the earie and see if I can pick up something."

"Another thing, Eddy. You know anything about the stock market?"

"All I know is, that's where they sell cows."

"Funny. But if you hear any noise about guys buying stock — securities, common stock — for Axel Scalzo, that would interest me greatly."

"Stock. Like in machine-gun factories, or bomb dumps, or — "

"Like a company called Universal Electronics, specifically."

"Crazy."

"Yeah. He's got a big hunk, and maybe some of his pals could be buying the stock, holding it in their names for him."

"What for?"

"Beats me."

"Yeah. Maybe he wants to be a tygoon, huh? Scalzo. What's with Scalzo?"

"I don't know. Maybe nothing. Just keep your ears flapping. You ever hear of any of these citizens? Ryder Tangier?"

"Never heard of him. He sounds like a foreign country."

"Julie Tangier? Matthew Wyndham?"

He shook his head.

"That's about it I'm kind of in a hurry on this — mainly Kay. Where'll I meet you?"

"Four o'clock now, huh? Give me three hours for the first go at it. I shall get slicked up in a new undershirt, and go forth in the city, then later — as is my usual Friday-eve custom — lap up some sauce at Scalzo's. So why not meet me there at seven?"

"O.K."

Among his other interests, Axel Scalzo owned a cheesy nightclub on Third Street, called the South Seas, and it was the Scalzo's to which Eddy referred. The South Seas attempted to capture the whole flavor of Polynesia with four papier-mâché palm trees, which failed utterly, and featured booze, steak and lobster, strippers five nights a week, and a new and spreading L.A, epidemic, "Amateur Strip Night," on Friday nights.

What had started as an intriguing experiment in one club had caught on and spread to half a dozen others, including the South Seas. It was just what the name implied: a night when gals, not professionals, but merely tomatoes with an urge to bump and grind a bit while exposing pink epidermis, could put on a show for the howling clientele. Gals, caught in the fever, had been known to leap from the audience, yanking things off in a fine frenzy. Or so I'd been told.

"That's right," I said, "this is Friday night, hey, Eddy? Amateur night?"

"Well, what do you know?" he said innocently. "Who'd of thunk it?"

Eddy, however, knew what he was doing. Because it was Friday, Scalzo's joint would be crammed with the light-fingered and heavy-handed gentry, many of them awash in booze to their armpits, and probably with tongues flapping loosely.

So, with the business at hand settled, I prepared to leave.

"Thanks for sendin' me to that last doctor, Scott," Eddy said. "Thanks for nothin'."

"He didn't help either, huh?"

Eddy referred to Dr. Paul Anson, a good friend of mine who lives just down the hall from me in the Spartan Apartment Hotel. Since you could usually tell what TV shows Eddy was watching by comparing their commercials with Eddy's symptoms, and since about half of Paul's expensive practice consists of giving pink, green, and blue placebos to well-heeled Hollywood hypochondriacs, when Sick Eddy developed twinging alarums in all eight of his sinus cavities, I suggested he start watching the U.S. Steel Hour and pay a visit, at my expense, to Dr. Paul Anson. That had been a couple months ago and I hadn't yet heard the result from Eddy. But he was damned sure I was going to hear about it now.

"Help?" he said in high dudgeon. "He's the kind of doctor takes your pulse and won't give it back. He like to of killed me. He give me a shot to cure me of something, then he give me a shot to cure me of the first shot. You want to know what I think? I think he give me a transfusing of embalm fluid. I been gettin' stiffer ever since I was there — "

"Eddy, there are times when medical science is helpless in the face of disasters like epidemics and earthquakes and Eddy Sly, but I'm sure Paul did his best — "

"Well, it wasn't good enough, Scott. In fact, it was worse than useless, like toilet paper with holes in it or deodorants made out of sweat. I come out sicker'n I went in. I know my days was numbered before, but he subtracted some — "

"Eddy," I said solemnly, "you're right."

"Huh?"

"You've convinced me. I imagine by now you're in such bad shape that if you got well the shock would kill you."

"Huh?" he said again, and I made it to the door.

I got it open and stepped outside before he recovered. As I started down the hall he was saying, "But, man, I don't dare walk through a cemetery; somethin' would reach out . . . " And then I was beyond earshot. Feeling great. It didn't drag me down when I saw Eddy; on the contrary, whenever I left Sick Eddy Sly, I left feeling healthy as hell.

Five

Still feeling very healthy, I drove up Santa Monica Boulevard to the Universal Electronics Building — which housed the executive offices and a large warehousing area — and parked in the lot. The building was low and new-looking, four or five feet of red brick at its base, beige stucco above that. Double doors at the building's left, lettered UNIVERSAL ELECTRONICS, INC., opened on a wide hallway and I stepped inside, my heels clicking softly on the floor's polished-cork surface.

Doors on both sides of the hallway were closed, but the nearest one on my left bore the name MR. MATTHEW WYNDHAM, PRESIDENT. I pushed it open and went in.

Went in and stopped. Made a noise much like the noise Eddy had made on awakening: "Waowoo," or word to that effect.

She — it was a woman, of course — sat behind a beige desk at the far side of the room, left of center, near a door leading to another office. On the right wall were filing cabinets, and on the left some charts, but this I noted only with the edges of my eyes, since the eye innards were straining at the tomato. A rust-blonde tomato, hair thick and growingly healthy, lips and eyes and what I could see of her above the desk all parts of a human heat wave. She glanced up at me, smiling, and bells rang. I thought, This is ridiculous, then realized the bell was merely a phone ringing somewhere, the sound issuing from the intercom on the lovely's desk.

I steamed forward over the carpet toward the smiling gat as her eyes widened and a voice said, "Hello . . . yes. This is Matt — " and then was cut off as the gal, in pretty confusion, flipped the intercom switch, grabbed a manila folder, and stood up.

"Darn, I forgot it *again*," she said, and walked toward the filing cabinets on my right, moving with the ripple and sway and woweewow seldom seen outside nudist camps. At the cabinet she said, "I'd forget my girdle . . . " and even before she completed the sentence, turning to glance at me again, I had thought, Who're you kidding? anticipating her conclusion, which naturally was: ". . . if I wore one."

She slipped the folder in the file and turned to face me. I grinned at her just on general principles — and the door in the back wall banged open. A guy came through it in a large hurry, stalking toward the hallway. I was between him and the exit, and he'd come out so fast he nearly ran into me. He stopped, gunned his eyes at me while his jaw sagged an inch, a short, wide, stubby guy with an expression almost like dismay on his pimpled chops. Then he zipped around me and out, slamming the door behind him.

The gal walked back to her desk, and I followed every inch every inch of the way, until she sat down and said, "May I help you with some assistance?"

Had I been calm, cool, sharp as a tack, and collected, something about those words might well have struck me as mildly warped. But at that moment I was not calm, cool, sharp as a tack, and collected.

I said, "The probability is astronomical. I'm Shell Scott—Are you Miss Brandt . . ."

I was looking at the name plate on her desk, naturally expecting to see the name of Wyndham's secretary, Alice Brandt, the gal I'd been told was built like a brick brick-factory, but the name plate said MISS DUDEN, so I let it finish sort of limply: " . . . Miss Duden?"

She laughed. "Are you Miss Brandt, Miss Duden? Now what kind of a question is that? How could Miss Brandt be me, or me — or is it I? — be, ah — "

"Yeah, let's forget it," I said. "My name is Shell Scott. I'd like to see Mr. Wyndham. O.K.?"

"Do you have an appointment?"

"Nope."

"I'll tell him you're here."

She flipped the intercom switch and said, "Mr. Wyndham, there's a Mr. Shell Scott here to see you."

After a three- or four-second pause a man's voice, the same one I'd heard before over the intercom, replied, "Well, all right, send him in. In one minute, Doody."

She flipped the intercom switch and smiled up at me. "That's me. Doody."

"I figured it was. What happened to Miss Brandt? Not that I mind —"

"Oh, she went away somewhere, three weeks ago, and I got her job. My first name's really Nell, but I can't stand the name Nell, can you?"

"Well — "

"I hate it. That's why everybody calls me Doody."

I thought that was smart. She sure didn't look like a Nell.

Doody went on, "That's why Mr. Wyndham called me Doody."

It was starting to be borne in upon me that considering this gal's stunning face and figure, perhaps the law of compensation had over-compensated when it came to the mental department of Doody.

Something she'd said, a phrase scattered among her remarks, stuck in my thoughts, and I was just going to ask what she'd meant by saying Miss Brandt had gone away somewhere, when Doody said, "I guess it's been a minute. You may go in now."

Well, questions would keep. I thanked her, went to the office door and inside.

Matthew Wyndham sat behind a brown desk, a desk with the total barrenness of paper or gewgaws which is supposed, I gather, to indicate fiendish application and activity, and nodded, smiling pleasantly as I came in.

"Mr. Scott?" he said. "I don't believe we've met, have we?"

The voice was rich and deep, and he had wavy gray hair over a handsome pink-cheeked face on which was the frank, open, friendly expression of a man who could sell Cadillacs to Volkswagen salesmen, or vice versa. He stood up and leaned over the desk as I approached, shaking my hand in a firm grip. He appeared to be in his middle fifties, about five feet, ten inches tall and thirty pounds overweight.

I smiled back at his neat white teeth and said, "No sir. I represent one of your stockholders, a man interested in investing a sizable amount in Universal Electronics."

"Oh? What is the man's name?"

"I'd prefer not to say, Mr. Wyndham. He's concerned primarily with the company's prospects, of course, the new products and the plans for expansion and distribution mentioned in your last annual report. Especially when you intend to introduce the new ultrasonic blender and miniaturized RDF we've been hearing about." I went on for another minute, asking questions and making comments which Gabriel Rothstein had said should make me sound like a man who knew what he was talking about. Then I finished it up, casually, "Naturally, too, he's concerned about any continuing effect the thievery by Ryder Tangier might have on the stock."

Wyndham listened patiently, attentively, and nodded when I stopped speaking. "Yes," he said quietly, "Ryder's — Mr. Tangier's — defalcation was a blow to all of us. Especially to me. For a month prior to the audit I had noticed Mr. Tangier's increasing nervousness and irritability, but assumed it was merely the press of work, creative tension. . . . However that's a closed chapter. I can assure you there's no possibility such a thing could happen again."

"You've never had any doubt of his guilt, then?"

"Doubt?" He looked mildly surprised. "Well, perhaps at first, but then . . . Of course, I did what I could for Ryder at the trial. Even spoke to the judge in hopes of leniency. I said I was sure the board, myself included, would welcome Mr. Tangier back as head of R and D if he could be given probation, and that I personally would guarantee the firm — that is, the stockholders — would suffer no similar loss in the future. It wasn't enough. . . . But I assume you're familiar with the result."

"Yes. Incidentally, I understand your secretary was a character witness for Mr. Tangier at the trial." I smiled and added pleasantly, "She didn't get fired because of that, did she?"

Wyndham laughed softly. "Goodness, no. I wanted her to stay. She quit suddenly, and I was quite at my wit's end until Doo — Miss Duden applied for the position." His eyes, unless I was imagining things, took on a rather hot and distant expression as he momentarily thought of "Doo — Miss Duden."

Then he blinked, his eyes came back, cooling, and he launched into a glowing description of Universal Electronics' rosy future, peppering his talk with facts and figures about price-earnings ratio, reduction of long-term debt, and a great deal of other gibberish.

He finished it up with, "While it is certainly true that Mr. Tangier was of great value to the company, I would say we still have, without him, an R-and-D section second to none in the entire industry. And, of course, many of the projects initiated by Mr. Tangier will be completed by others. No, Mr. Scott, rest assured that Universal Electronics is on the threshold of its greatest successes."

He was a man of enthusiasm, no doubt about it. I got the impression that if there'd been a UE pennant handy, he'd have grabbed it and marched around the room, waving it wildly. He leaned over and stabbed the switch on his intercom and said, "Doo — Miss Duden, bring me file sixteen, please."

"Right away, Mr. Wyndham."

In a few seconds the door opened and the gorgeous rust-blonde gal scurried in from the outer office, the free play of numerous forces, not one of which seemed to include gravity, testifying en masse to her total absence of girdles and other such crutches, and while I am a guy who almost never fails to devote his entire attention to glorious vistas such as that, I had sense enough or will power enough to give part of my attention to Matthew Wyndham.

Yeah, his eyes did that thing again. He watched every ripple and flurry and supercharged undulation with the intentness of a dedicated scientist finding a brand-new bug under his microscope. I'll tell you, roughly, what it was like. In another, earlier, time, it would have been a look accompanied by grunting noises, the flaring of nostrils, and the swinging of a stone ax on the top of her conk.

Doody deposited a manila folder on Wyndham's desk, then headed for the door. There she turned jazzily and said, "Will there be anything else tonight, Mr. Wyndham?"

"Anything else? Ah, no, no, that's all." He glanced at his watch. "You may go, Doo — " He just left it hanging there.

As the door closed behind her, I commented on a framed photo I'd noticed on his desk. It was of a middle-aged woman, with the sort of face you see on English butlers, and two teen-agers, a boy and a girl. "Your family, Mr. Wyndham?" I said, indicating the photo.

"What? Oh . . . yes." He shook himself like a dog coming out of a lake. "Yes, indeed. My wife, Maude, and our two youngsters. Are you married, Mr. Scott?"

"No." I smiled. "Still a bachelor."

"A bachelor, eh? Um . . . " He rolled that "um" around for a bit, as if extracting all possible flavor from it.

So while he was occupied with rolling it around, I said pleasantly, "One other thing. Do you have any idea why Mr. Scalzo is attracted to UE stock?"

"Who?"

"Mr. Scalzo. Axel Scalzo."

He shook his head. "I don't believe I know anybody of that name. Scalzo?"

"Yeah. Well, he owns a pretty good chunk of the company's stock."

"Indeed."

He blinked, and fell silent. And I decided that was about enough of the interview for today. I assumed that John Kay must have come here to talk with Matthew Wyndham too, but I didn't want to bring it up myself. It appeared that Mr. Wyndham wasn't going to mention it either. But he fooled me.

"You know," he said slowly, "your comments remind me of something. Oddly enough, you're the second detective to mention the name Scalzo to me. The other was here, oh, a week or so ago." His forehead furrowed slightly as he reached into memory. "Mr. Kay I think it was." He paused. "Who is this gentleman Scalzo?"

"He isn't a gentleman. Never mind. I just thought I'd ask."

Mr. Wyndham's remarks about Kay had surprised and puzzled me a bit. Not because he'd mentioned Kay's name. It was just that I had not told Mr. Wyndham that *I* was a detective.

He looked at his wife's photo again, then at his watch. "I hope I've been of service, Mr. Scott. But I must leave the office now." Perhaps it sounded a bit abrupt, because he relaxed somewhat and smiled pleasantly again. "Dinner-dance at the club, you know. Promised my wife a little outing. And if I'm late again . . . " He did not finish telling me what would happen, but my impression was that Mrs. Wyndham would, in that case, do something extremely nauseating to Mr. Wyndham.

I stood up and we shook hands. I said, "Thank you very much, Mr. Wyndham. You've been quite helpful."

I went out, closing the door behind me. Doody was across the room near a small closet, slipping a cream-colored coat on over her pale-green knit suit. She headed for the hallway door as I reached it, so I held it open and said, "All through?"

"All through. Thank you." She swept past me, a scent of delicate perfume titillating my nostrils. I followed my nostrils, letting them flare all they wanted to.

Understand, I do not let my penchant for gorgeous females interfere with my total dedication to the job at hand. At least, not often. Certainly not all the time. And it is undeniably true that in many cases, when it is necessary to investigate a clam-mouthed company executive or too-secretive businessman, much more of value can be mulcted from the said businessman's secretary than from the man himself. The personal secretary usually knows all sorts of interesting things about the boss and, properly approached, sometimes will tell all sorts of interesting things about the boss.

True, Doody had been with Wyndham only three weeks, she'd said, but she might have learned a lot in three weeks, a lot that I should know. Clearly, I would be remiss in my duty if I did not mulct all the information I could out of Doody. And, if you could have seen her walking down the hallway a mere three or four feet ahead of me, you would have agreed with me 100 per cent.

So I quickened my pace, drew abreast — or at least alongside — of Doody and said, "We didn't really get a chance to talk much, Miss Duden. May I buy you a drink, or dinner, while we — "

"That *would be* fun." I blinked. I hadn't actually told her what we were going to do. "And don't call me Miss Duden," she went on. "I don't like that either. Call me Doody."

"Yeah, sure." We'd passed through the front doors and were on Santa Monica Boulevard, so I grinned at her and said, "Well, let's . . . do it now, hey?"

"That's the spirit," she said. "Like that old maximum, don't put off today what you can do tomorrow."

This time the warp twanged in my ear a little. I ran over it once, trying to take it apart, but it seemed to have come unglued before I got to it. So I merely shrugged and said, "To say the minumum. You know any place handy where we can start with a cocktail?"

"You can start with a cocktail anywhere. There's the Matador."

"The what?"

She pointed. Across the street was the glass-and-black-marble front of a cocktail lounge. Over the door was a large neon bullfighter, waving a red cape with a stiff awkwardness that surely would have gotten him gored in the ring. A sign gaudily announced that it was indeed the MATADOR.

"Great," I said, and steered her toward it.

Inside we found a booth and ordered drinks. I had my usual bourbon-and-water, and Doody ordered one of those gooey feminine concoctions. It was green, with a little froth on it, and looked like something that had been bitten by a rattlesnake. I glanced around at colorful serapes, painted gourds, bullfight posters, and wide-brimmed straw hats on the walls.

Then I raised my glass and said, "*Salud y amor y pesetas,*" quoting part of one of my favorite Mexican toasts.

She smiled. "Oh . . . *parlez-vous Español?*" she asked brightly.

"No, it's just a toast I — what?"

"Well, let's drown the hatch," she said, and had a swallow of her drink. I had a healthy gulp of mine. And the conversation for a minute or two went along at the same dizzy pace. At the end of the minute or two I had become totally convinced: Doody, clearly, was not the brightest babe in the world. But I was also convinced I didn't really give a hoot. She was animated, happy, bubbling with laughter, her beige-brown eyes sparkling, lips softly curling. Her voice was a little too high, with a slightly twanging nasality that might have been annoying issuing from lips less provocatively incandescent, but there was a sweetness in it that made the sound almost pleasant. And too, every once in a while she took a deep breath before unleashing a gush of conversation, and when Doody took: a deep breath it relegated intelligence to a series of numbers like 38-22-36.

I stubbed out my smoke and reached for another, finding the pack empty. So I excused myself and walked to the cigarette machine at the bar's end, where there was also a glassed-in phone booth. As I got a fresh pack of smokes I noticed a man in the booth just dropping a dime into the slot.

It was the guy-in-a-hurry, the stubby character who'd nearly bumped into me when leaving Wyndham's office. So, curiously, I watched from just outside the booth as he dialed, 988-4584. He put the phone to his ear, glanced around — and looked right at me. His jaw went down and up again as it had in Wyndham's office, and he very suddenly hung up.

He stepped out and smiled tightly, as if his teeth were coming loose. "Busy," he said without conviction, then stood there watching me.

I entered the booth, dialed my office number, let the phone ring a few times and hung up. I stepped out and said, "Nobody there."

Back at our table I said to Doody, "Remember the guy who charged out of Mr. Wyndham's office just as I arrived?"

She nodded.

"Who is he?"

"He said his name was Mr. Foster."

"Had he been there before?"

"Not that I know of. I don't think I'd ever seen him before. Why?"

"Just curious. Had he been with Wyndham long?"

"No, he came in just a minute or two before you did. He seemed in a hurry, didn't he?"

"Yeah," I said, wondering why. And wondering why he'd reacted so peculiarly both times he'd seen me.

He was in the phone booth again now, making a call, looking toward me — or Doody, or maybe both of us — from time to time. When he came out he had a drink at the bar and then left.

I said to Doody, "What's Wyndham's phone number?" She told me, but it wasn't the one Foster had dialed. Doody said she didn't know whose number it was. "Why don't you call it and ask them?"

"A capital idea," I said, and did just that. But nobody answered, so I went back to Doody.

She was hungry — as was I, for that matter, having had no chow today except my breakfast mush, which is nutritious, but so lousy the way I cook it that I seldom eat much of it, and which had been so lousy this morning I hadn't eaten any of it. So we ordered dinner. My choice was an extra-thick cut of prime ribs, as rare as I could get it, and Doody had a crab Louie.

While we ate I brought the conversation around to Universal Electronics, her boss, Matthew Wyndham, and allied subjects. She had a good word for everything and everybody, which wasn't much help to me, since I was looking for bad words. Doody asked me what kind of work I did, and since Wyndham already knew I was a detective there seemed no harm in telling her. After that she seemed more interested in asking me about my work than in answering my questions, an attitude widely touted as a way to Win Friends and Influence People, but again not of much help to me.

Finally I said, "I guess the Ryder Tangier thing was long before your time."

"Oh, yes. He's the man who stole the money, isn't he?"

"Allegedly."

"What does that mean?"

"Well, he's alleged to have embezzled the loot — he was accused of it, anyway."

"He must have done it then, mustn't he? They sent him to prison, I thought."

"That's right. He's in the clink now."

"Well, I don't know anything about that. It all happened while Miss Brandt was working for Mr. Wyndham."

"Uh-huh. Incidentally, you told me she went away somewhere. Where'd she go?"

"I don't know, exactly. We've been friends for over two years — we both lived at the Lanai Apartments on Sunset, that's where we met — and Alice told me she was going to quit her job and go back east. Her family is back there, I think."

"Where back east?"

"Just back east, that's all she said, and there's a lot of it back there. Anyway, she said if I applied for the position I'd probably get it — if she knew Mr. Wyndham. Whatever that meant."

I had a hunch I knew what that meant.

Doody went on, "So I applied for the job and got it. Was *I* surprised! I can type and all that, but I don't know much about electron things. Mr. Wyndham said it didn't make much difference, isn't that funny?"

Eying Doody's other-than-typing talents, and recalling my impression of Matthew Wyndham, it didn't strike me as particularly funny, certainly not hilarious. I said, "This Alice Brandt was rather attractive, wasn't she?"

"Oh, yes. But she's an older woman. She must have been . . . maybe thirty."

Thirty is *my* age. I said, a bit stiffly, "That's not exactly what I — "

"But she was remarkably well preserved, as the saying goes. She looked a little bit like me, only older of course. I mean, she's blonde and not skinny or anything."

Not skinny or anything. If that was how Doody thought of herself, it was good enough for me. Miss Brandt must have been a wow. Another blonde too. As I recalled, the photo of Mrs. Wyndham had been of a gal with hair the color of mice. Was this a clue?

And, idly thinking in that fashion, a rather peculiar sequence of events struck me. Ryder Tangier had been sent to Q a month ago. A week later — about three weeks ago, when Doody got her job with Wyndham — Miss Alice Brandt quit and "went back east." At approximately the same time, Julie Tangier had simply disappeared from the Watson-Parker. I didn't know what significance that had, if any, but it left me with a mild uneasiness. An uneasiness accented by the undeniable fact that John Kay had been killed only yesterday.

"Doody," I said, "you meet everybody who calls on Wyndham, don't you? Before they go in to see him?"

She nodded. "Yes. That's part of what I'm hired for, to make appointments and like that."

"Do you remember a man named John Kay calling on Mr. Wyndham?"

She frowned again, and got the intent expression that told me she was thinking hard about it. I said, "He was a detective, though he might not have said so. A man about fifty — "

"Oh, him. The other detective." Her face brightened. "Yes, I remember him now. He came to see Mr. Wyndham . . . about a week or so ago. Thursday or Friday, I think it was. And again this last Wednesday."

Wednesday. And he'd been killed Thursday. Which could have been a coincidence,

"One other thing," I said. "How often does Axel Scalzo come around to see Mr. Wyndham?"

"Who?"

"Axel Scalzo. He's been in to see Mr. Wyndham, hasn't he?"

She shook her head. "Not that I know of. I don't even remember that name from anywhere."

Doody had that hard-thinking-and-intent expression on again. "Why are you asking me all these questions?" she said suspiciously. "About this detective, and Mr. Wyndham, and Alice and all. I thought you wanted to buy me a drink — like it's romantic, or something." Her voice went up the scale two notes. "If you think you can ply me with drinks and undermine my loyalty — "

"It was only one drink, and there wasn't anything in it except some green — "

". . . and ply me with crab Louies while you put the wool in my eyes, well, you've got another think — "

"Doody, please. Relax. We'll talk about anything *you* want to talk about."

"Well." Her face smoothed a bit. "All right. Then why are you asking all those questions?"

"Uh," I said. "Well, I represent a large stockholder, interested in the company." I repeated much of what I'd said to Matthew Wyndham, adding, "But enough of that. Let's talk about you. Us. About the glorious future beckoning — "

"So. You invited me to drink and dinner so you could ply me — "

"Doody, dammit — "

"Well, didn't you? Tell me the truth."

Why did she have to put it that way? I took a deep breath, looked at her narrowed eyes, and said, "Yes."

Silence. She looked, I thought, a little hurt. After a moment I went on, "At least that was part of the reason. There was another part, Doody. And how there was another part! And if you can't figure that part out by yourself, then none of the superlatives on the tip of my tongue would convince you."

Slowly her narrowed eyes went back to normal, and a small smile finally curved those wild red lips. "All right," she said. "Then let's say good-bye to the bygones, and all that."

"Fine, Doody, let's . . . let's do what?"

"Actually," she said, "when you came into the office, I thought, 'Boy, there's a big one.' I mean, you must be two hundred pounds if you're an inch, and I don't like a man who's too perfect, anyway."

"You don't, huh?" I considered that more, liking it less. "I'm not sure I know precisely what that means. . . ."

"You know, you came in like you owned the place, or were going to wreck it maybe, and besides, you look like a man who's *lived*, you know. Maybe too much."

I kept trying to get a big boost from her complimentary remarks; but I couldn't quite make it. I sat there with, I guess, a kind of dull hope on my face, a hope that was not to be fulfilled, as she went on,

"Some women like handsome men, the almost pretty type, but give me a big wreck any old time."

Well, I thought. Well! I realize that I'm no Cary Grant or dashing Rip Cord, idol of teen-agers; and that my nose has been broken a couple of times and a little tiny bit shot off the top of my left ear; and that I have been clobbered in and about my chops by everything from eight knuckles at once to the flat side of a meat cleaver; and that I do indeed bear a few little scars, most of which are not visible — at least not when I'm sitting in a nightclub with a big-mouthed tomato — but a wreck?

Suddenly I realized Doody was laughing silently, her light-brown eyes squinting merrily and small gay sounds issuing from her lips. "Oh, you should see your expression!" she said in sheer delight.

"I've had quite enough jazz about my expression, Miss," I said loftily.

"Oh! I'll ruin my mascara." She plucked at a paper tissue and dabbed at her eyes.

"Fine," I said. "That's fine with me — "

"Oh, Shell," she said. "Shellie. That'll teach you to ply me with things, and play fast and loose with me."

Maybe she wasn't so dumb after all. I said, "I wasn't exactly plying you, Miss Duden. And as for playing fast and loose with you . . . uh, Doody, that's another story. What do you mean, fast and loose?"

"Oh, you men. All you can see is — the outside. Beauty is only skin deep, you know."

"Baby, that's deep enough."

"You know what I mean. A woman is more than sixty-five cents' worth of chemicals, or whatever the scientists say."

"I never said it. Man — I mean lady — Doody, I didn't even know it was sixty-five — I mean, let's start over."

She laughed and said something I simply didn't understand at all. And that's the way it went. We finished dinner, had coffee, and soon were standing next to the table as Doody said, "Thanks *so* much, Shellie. I forgive you for being so mean. I do have to run."

My head was whirling. When you're used to logic, and when you try very hard to pursue trains of thought to their logical conclusions but instead wind up with train wrecks, and when this is accompanied by the sight of the disturbingly physical lovelinesses of a Doody, it is inevitable that your head will start whirling.

43

So I said, "It's been grand. Yes. We'll have to do this again, whatever we did. In fact, if I didn't have to work tonight, maybe we could do it tonight — "

"Oh, but I have a date tonight. Didn't I tell you? Or is that what you meant? Anyway, I do have to run." She smiled up at me. "I didn't mean all the things I said." Then she reached up and patted my cheek with cool, soft fingers, patted gently, smiling wondrously, and said, "Anyway, you're a *nice* old wreck."

And was gone.

I stood there for a few seconds. Then I sat down in the booth again. The shape I was in, it just wouldn't do for me to go out into the world. Not just yet.

"Waiter," I said, as he walked by, "please bring me another drink."

What had happened, really? Well, for one thing, I'd spent a lot more time telling her about me and what I was doing than in learning from her the intimate and possibly sinister secrets of Universal Electronics and such vital matters.

But I had learned that Doody, though perhaps not overly familiar with what some refer to as "the intellectual life," knew quite enough about plain old life, knew a lot, one hell of a lot, about men.

And I had learned that very cool fingers could nonetheless leave a very warm brand on a man's cheek.

I finished my drink. Then, almost back to normal, I went out into the real world again.

Six

Shortly before 7 P.M., I parked the Cad on Third near the South Seas, checked the .38 Colt Special I was wearing under my tan coat, then stuck the gun back into its clamshell holster and got out of the car.

Sick Eddy hadn't had much time to pick anything important off the underworld wireless, but he was good; he knew the places to listen, and when and where to speak, so I figured there was a fifty-fifty chance he'd have something of interest to me.

I had checked the gun, not because I was going to meet Eddy Sly but because I was going into the South Seas — the joint owned by Axel Scalzo.

Not that there was any real reason to expect trouble — certainly not at this point in my budding investigation of Universal Electronics. So far there wasn't the slightest trace of any connection between Scalzo and Wyndham or other UE people. Possibly I'd put too much emphasis on the simple fact that Scalzo had been buying a lot of UE stock. But going armed and somewhat warily into Scalzo's dive was what Doody — in one of the remarks I was beginning to think of as her "Doodyisms" — might have called the pound of prevention.

Not only was there a chance I'd run into Axel Scalzo himself in the South Seas, but I knew that a number of unsavory characters — along with, and unsuspected by, the normal night-clubbing solid citizens of the area — liked to drop into the place, either alone or with buddies or babes, for a drink or several. Especially on Friday nights, since the hoodlums among us enjoy the sway of before or swing of behind just as much as the non-hoodlums among us, and sometimes even more so. Consequently I might come face to face with characters whom I had previously met in circumstances that could by no stretch of the imagination be called enjoyable, characters who would probably object to my presence, and even to my existence.

Then there was Scalzo himself, of course. I've mentioned that we'd never tried killing each other, or come to blows, but whenever we got close, even though not a word was spoken, people around us seemed to sort of edge away, like extras in Western movies when the gunfighters start stalking toward each other down the dusty street. It was as if they unconsciously knew something calamitous was likely to happen, but just hadn't happened. Not yet.

If Scalzo was around tonight I wouldn't have any trouble spotting him. He was maybe six feet and about my weight, with a high forehead that went clear to the back of his neck, very large gray eyes, and sort of pinkish eyebrows. I guess he'd once been a redhead before all his hair had absconded with his waves, and he had the fair, sun-tender complexion of many redheads. He had a long, narrow chin that seemed to dangle and he sort of kept his lips pushed together like a guy with his mouth full of spit. Whenever he opened his mouth to say something stupid I expected a bunch of drool to puddle out. You get the picture: no more charm than a hyena.

He was a surprisingly mild and soft-spoken cat, but his purr could be deadly; he had claws. Without proof, I guessed he was responsible for at least two or three murders in the city of L.A., and numerous lesser crimes. Actually, most of what I thought about Scalzo was conjecture, opinion without evidence approaching proof, because the man was unlike most of those I considered hard-core hoods in that he was remarkably clean — that is, his record was. As a kid he'd done a bit for stealing an auto, but since then there'd been only one arrest — for allegedly fixing a horse race four years ago — and no convictions. He moved with "good people," as well as numerous shady characters, drank and dined at the best spots, owned a good deal of property, and occasionally spoke at testimonial dinners for one politician or another.

He wasn't actually considered a gangster or syndicate man — except maybe by me and a few police officers in the Intelligence Division — but he had a wide acquaintance not only among certain political operators and respectable people, but also among the lower strata of city life, the creeps and heavies who pull the jobs, carry the guns, heist the loot, and bop people on their skulls. Some of the latter, undoubtedly, would be in the South Seas tonight.

The club was on a corner lot. The entrance was at an angle so that it faced the intersection, and was reached by walking down a narrow path under a green awning. Australian tree ferns and a few scraggly banana trees grew on both sides of the path. Inside, I let my eyes grow adjusted to the dimness, then walked to the long bar paralleling the left wall for half the club's length. Farther back, on the right, was a piano bar with stools around it, and the rest of the room — except for a small dance floor before a bandstand at the club's rear — was crammed with little round tables. Four papier-mâché palm trees — thin, so they wouldn't obstruct the view at show time — sprouted in the room like large, rangy artificial flowers.

Seven o'clock was early for the South Seas — the show didn't begin until 9 P.M. — and only a few customers were visible in the dimness, most of them at the long bar. I didn't see Eddy.

When the bartender stopped in front of me I ordered a bourbon-and-water in a tall glass. I didn't really want a drink but needed something to play with until Eddy showed. Fifteen minutes later I'd finished the long highball but there was still no sign of Eddy Sly. And that puzzled me.

Eddy was a good many things he shouldn't have been, but one of the things I liked about the guy was that he did what he said he'd do. He had always kept his word, at least to me, and when he'd said he would meet me here at seven, I knew he had fully intended to be here at seven.

Apparently he'd been delayed unexpectedly — assuming, of course, that he'd gotten out of his room in the first place. If he'd fallen asleep with a sock in his hand, Eddy was going to be damned rudely awakened.

I slid off my stool, went out the club's entrance, and trotted to my Cad. Two minutes later I'd parked in the lot next to the Gable Hotel and was taking the stairs three at a time to the third floor. Eddy's room was 304. I stopped in front of it, raised my hand to knock — and stopped. There were muffled sounds from inside, not the sounds of a man tossing in his sleep. And there were soft voices, more than one. Then there was a solid smack, unmistakably the sound of a hand or fist striking flesh.

I felt the muscles tensing in my back, thigh tendons tightening. I pulled the .38 from under my coat, put a hand on the doorknob, and turned it easily. The door was locked. And suddenly all sound inside the room stopped.

Somebody in there must have noticed the knob turning.

The rest of it I did without much thought; it just happened.

Whoever was inside the room already knew somebody was standing in the hallway. So I knocked a jazzy tattoo on the door and stepped back to the middle of the hallway, saying, "Hey, Eddy, you home?" and then lunged forward, slamming my right foot against the door near the lock. The jar ran from my heel up to my spine and kind of lifted my head a little, but the wood splintered and the door flew open. My momentum carried me into the room, bent forward and stumbling. There was a lot of movement in the room right then, but for a moment it was all sharp and clear in my eyes.

On the bed at my left sprawled Eddy Sly, his face raised toward me — a puffed and bloody face. Redness glistening from his nose to his chin made his mouth look like hamburger drowned in ketchup. Near him stood a short wide-shouldered stocky man half turned toward me. A second man was at the right side of the room, his body half out an open window, feet touching the fire-escape. I got a quick, vivid impression of black-browed dark eyes, a sharp nose, thick lips with an angled red scar in the upper one. In his right hand he held a heavy automatic pistol. The gun was aimed toward the floor but as I burst in he flipped it up toward me.

I let my weight drop, trying to grab the carpet as the automatic blasted, the sound so loud it was almost like a solid blow. Before I hit the floor something slapped my hip, then my chin and chest bounced on the carpet. As I skidded forward I got my right arm stuck out toward the window and fired twice, rolling onto my side. I didn't even hit the window, much less the man scrambling backward out of it; both my slugs smacked into the plastered wall. I rolled completely over, came up onto my knees.

The man near the bed was in a slight crouch now. His hand came away from his hip, light glancing from metal. The gun was pointed at my body, the man's elbow pressed against his right hip, when I fired. He was good enough, and fast, but not quite fast enough.

I fired three times. I saw his left ear disintegrate, part of it suddenly gone; then I saw a hole leap into his left cheek. His head snapped back. My third slug tore into the soft flesh beneath his chin, then sliced through his brain and hit the solid bone of his skull. He straightened, was lifted upward two or three inches, as if he'd been hit by a hammer.

He seemed to hang there, like a man suspended from a hook. I snapped my gun toward the window and fired again. My aim was better, much better than before; only nobody was there. I heard the clatter of feet on the fire escape's metal rungs. On my left the man I'd shot was falling. I jerked my head back in time to see him crumple, almost gently, to the floor. There didn't seem to be any sound at all now, just the memory of shockingly loud gunshots.

Eddy stared at me and moved a hand — very slowly, it seemed — over the smear of blood on his mouth. I jumped to the window, leaned out. I heard him running before I saw him. A big man in tan jacket, brown trousers, bareheaded, racing toward a car parked at the alley's end. I sighted over the Colt's short barrel, aimed at the middle of the tan jacket, and squeezed the trigger. Only a click this time. The gun was empty. He jumped into the car, a gray Chrysler, and was gone. I didn't get the license number. I'd never seen the man before. But I'd know that face if I saw it again.

I pulled my head back into the room, stuck my empty gun into its clamshell holster, walked over to the bed. Eddy was sitting up now. He wore a gray suit, white shirt, stringy blue tie. Blood smeared the tie and stained the white shirt.

"Waowoo," he said.

His left hand rested in his lap, two of the fingers twisted, obviously broken. The whiteness of snapped bone showed through the torn flesh of his second finger.

"Eddy," I said, "you all right? You O.K.?"

He ran his good hand over his mouth again, smearing away most of the blood. Then he looked straight at me, scowling, and said, "What in hell kind of question is that?"

I grinned. It wasn't the kindest thing to do under the circumstances, but Eddy's remark snapped the tension in me. Eddy's characteristic — almost healthy — comment shifted time and space back to normal.

"Boy," Eddy went on, "am I sick! Man, they beat hell out of me. I know I got internal injuries. I can feel somethin' oozin' around my spleen. . . ."

I let him talk. If Eddy was moaning about his fatal wounds, it was at least eight to five that he had no fatal wounds. So now I took another look at the dead man, wondering.

Wondering about a lot of things. Because, though I hadn't known the guy who'd beat it out through the window, I knew the guy who'd left through the top of his skull. He had a macerated ear, a hole in his cheek, and a cave furrowed through his brain, but the features were unmistakably the same.

The guy Doody had called Foster.

Foster, the stubby cat who had almost bumped into me when I'd first seen him, when he'd been leaving Matthew Wyndham's office in such a hurry.

Odd, it was. Three times I'd seen him, and each time he had gawked at me with an expression of vast surprise — when he'd burst from Wyndham's office, when he'd eyeballed me at the phone booth, and finally just now when I'd crashed through Eddy's door. From the birth of our acquaintance to its death, surprise, surprise, surprise.

I had, of course, wondered why; maybe now I was getting an inkling.

Seven

I'd put in a call to the complaint board, told my story, and asked that an ambulance be sent to the Gable Hotel. A call would be out on the gray Chrysler, but I didn't expect any help there.

In the meantime Eddy had washed his face, and except for a split lip and several lumps, plus the two broken fingers, he seemed little worse than usual.

I said, "What happened, Eddy? All of it, from the beginning."

"I come back here about quarter to seven," he said. "Was gonna put on my good rags before going to the South Seas. Them muzzlers was here waitin' for me."

"You know them?"

"Don't know this creep," he said, nodding toward the man on the floor, "but the other bird is a butcher been hangin' around with Scalzo and his boys the last couple months. Don't know what he's called."

"Scalzo, huh? That's interesting. What'd they want?"

"That's the kicker. They wanted to know what *you* wanted."

"How'd they know I'd been talking to you, Eddy? You didn't accidentally let that drop to anybody this afternoon, did you?"

"You think I'm nuts or somethin'? After you was here I hit some of the joints, and sat around in Casey's book for a while, jawed with some of the boys. But I sure as hell didn't mention you." He touched his lips, then probed various portions of his anatomy, grimacing and making weak sounds. "First damn thing them two muzzlers asks me when I got back here — after they bashed me a couple times — was what you was talkin' to me about, what was it you'd been after. And, bang, right off the bat, they asks me if you'd mentioned John Kay."

"Had you dropped his name to them, Eddy?"

51

"I hadn't said a peep but 'ow' till then. They asked me who you were working for, and if it was somebody called Gabriel Rothstein — who I never heard of. Well, Scott, about then I told them everything they wanted to know, and maybe even made up some. As long as I was talking they stopped pounding on me. So we got no secrets from those boys — the one left, anyways. I'm sorry — "

"Never mind that, Eddy. Just give me the rest of it."

"Well, I spilled my guts, kidneys, and gall bladder, and they kept asking me more, and finally they says, 'did Scott say anything about Ardis Ames?'"

"Who?"

"That's what I said. I said, 'Who?' and they said, 'Ardis Ames, god-damn you, you fink,' and unpleasant things like that, and I said, 'Man, you got me hung on one I can't get off of, I never heard of the bag.' So they dropped that, and tried to tear off a couple of my fingers, and start-ed over the whole bit again. I had begun to fear for my knockers when you come flyin' through the door like Peter Pan." He groaned again and said, "I feel faint. I think I'm dyin', Scott. I think I'm startin' to go. . . ."

"Hang on, Eddy. I can hear the siren now." The unearthly wail was faint, but getting louder.

"I guess I'll have to go to the hospital, huh?" he said hopefully.

"Oh, sure. You'll have to get those fingers set, if nothing else."

"What do you mean, if nothing else? Man, I'll bet they got to oper-ate. Every time I check into a hospital, the docs shake their heads and say, 'Well, we're gonna have to operate,' like they'll lose their license to practice if they don't get some of my insides out." He shook his head sadly. "There ain't much left in me, though, I'll tell you. Not any more. The sawbones done everything to me but take out my female organs — and I think they hunted for them. Scott, one doc was even tryin' to cut off my hypochondria. I told him, you lay one hand on it and I'll — "

"Eddy," I interrupted, "have you told me all that happened with those two guys?"

"Yeah, you got it."

"How about earlier? You pick anything off the wire?"

"Not a damn thing."

"That's pretty good. If Foster and his pal had left you alone, I'd still be in the dark. But instead they spread a little light, for which I thank the live one and the dead one."

"You mean their comin' here and half murdering me helped you out?"

"It helped plenty."

"That's nice. That's wonderful. I'll go get myself killed so you'll be *real* happy — "

"You know what I mean. I'll make this up to you, Eddy."

I'd been sitting on the side of the bed. Now I stood up and said, "Oof. What the hell?" I had experienced a sharp shooting pain where people sometimes get sharp shooting pains. I clapped a hand to my hip and it came away with blood on the fingers.

Just sitting talking to Eddy I hadn't felt any pain, but now I remembered that first shot from the guy in the window and something slapping my hip. It had, of course, been the bullet from the man's gun.

"Yeah," Eddy said. "I got to admit you sure stuck your neck out, coming in here like that." He chuckled. "How about that? You stuck your neck out and got shot in the — "

He stopped as feet pounded down the hallway outside. The siren had sighed to a stop a few seconds earlier; this would be the police, and ambulance attendants.

The wound Eddy had been referring to wasn't serious, and would hardly affect my walking. But it was damned embarrassing. And that black-browed, scar-lipped slob was going to be mightily embarrassed when I caught up with him.

I opened the door and let the people in.

When the routine was about finished, and Eddy was preparing to leave for Central Receiving Hospital — and I had a neat bandage covering my embarrassment — I said to him, "Thanks again, Eddy. I'll check with you later. Seriously, how do you feel now? Think you're going to be all right?"

He considered the question soberly, mentally rummaging around from point to point inside himself, then looked at me. "I guess so, Scott." He sighed. "I guess there's always a chance of livin', as long as you're still dyin'."

I grinned at him. "Spoken like a true optimist," I said, and left.

When you drive from L.A. out Beverly Boulevard, just before you reach the Beverly Hills city limits you come to several acres of green lawn and lavishly landscaped grounds, in the midst of which is a large, low, white building set back about a hundred yards from the street. That is the Beverly Club, which will welcome anybody as a member — if he is in the painful tax brackets, is nominated by three members, is not blackballed by anybody, and welcomes the opportunity to pay an initiation fee of four thousand dollars and dues of five hundred clams a year. It may amuse you to know that I'd never even been *this* close to the place before. This close being the white-cement driveway, headed for the entrance.

In talking to Doody over our prime ribs and crab Louie, part of the idle conversation had been about Matthew Wyndham, and his comment that he was taking his wife to a dinner-dance at the club. Doody had mentioned that his club was the Beverly, which explained why I was here for the first time in my life.

I left the Cad with an attendant near the club's entrance, walked up three wide steps and along a petunia-bordered path to enormous double doors with a carved letter *B* on each, through them and into the murmuring, heady richness of the Inside of the Beverly Club. Music floated in the air — a lot of strings and muted brass playing "How About You?" I walked ahead over spongy carpet, down a short hallway, and into a large room.

On my right was a bar, curving around the corner and out of sight. Farther right I could see the edge of a dance floor, black-suited men dancing with women in long, colorful, and flowing gowns. The men wore dinner jackets. I had stopped at my apartment for a shower and shave and a fresh suit — black, nicely tailored, and worn with a silver-white tie — but I had no fancy lapels, no little black tie. I might get tossed out of here yet.

Ahead and to my left were tables covered with pale-pink cloths. At most of them members or guests were seated, many of them eating. From here, counting the little slice of dance floor I could see, I guessed a hundred people or more were in view. I looked around but didn't see Matthew Wyndham.

A red-jacketed waiter walked by me carrying a silver tray laden with undersized chickens and I stopped him.

"Where'll I find Mr. Wyndham?" I asked him.

"Mr. Matthew Wyndham?" He was looking with disapproval at my plain old black two-hundred-dollar threads. "He is with Mrs. Wyndham, at a table overlooking the fountain." He indicated with a gentle glance the general area in which were the tables that overlooked the fountain.

Then he just stood there, eying me dreamily, as if I was supposed to give him a C-note or something. So I smiled at him, in friendly fashion, and said, "Real tasty-looking little chickens you've got there."

He sneered at me. "These," he said loftily, "are Malayan hens, stuffed with wild rice."

I let myself be suitably impressed. "Real wild rice, huh?"

His expression went clunk, and I left him there and walked to the tables overlooking the fountain. Since I am a detective, I found the table in something under five minutes. First I had to find the fountain, which was outside in the yard and consisted of three sprays of water shooting up into the air a foot. Near the window were a dozen tables from which this exciting display could be admired, and there were stern-faced women at many of them, and at one a woman sitting alone. I deduced that the woman alone was Mrs. Wyndham, because she looked like an English butler suffering from acute indigestion, and also — if you want the truth — because I asked another waiter.

Then I approached the table.

"Mrs. Wyndham?" I said.

She lifted her head and looked at me from little, frosty eyes. Then, having gotten a good look at me, she lifted her head some more and examined me with her nostrils.

"I am she," she said, and that told me almost more than I desired to know about Mrs. Wyndham.

"Well," I said, "you may never have heard of Sheldon Scott, but I am he. And he is very desirous of conversing with Mr. Wyndham."

I thought I'd carried that off rather well, but she said, "Who?"

"Mr. Wyndham. Is he anywhere about?"

"My word," she said.

I waited. Something had to happen. If nothing else, I'd just stand here and wear her down. The band finished "Laura," and swung into "Tease Me."

"My husband is at the bar," she said finally, in the manner of a woman saying "He has gone to hell." She moved her nostrils. "With that tall gentleman in the outrageous clothing."

I spotted Wyndham at the far end of the bar, talking to a tall, slim guy about thirty-five years old. The outrageous clothing consisted of a black suit and a silver-white tie. I said, "Thank you, Mrs. Wyndham. Who is the chap in the sports outfit?"

"I have no idea," she said. "I have never seen him before." She paused. "If you intend to speak with Mr. Wyndham, tell him to return to this table immediately."

"Yes, ma'am," I said, and walked toward the bar.

Wyndham and the tall, thin guy were in earnest conversation as I approached them. Wyndham's back was toward me, but the other man saw me coming and I heard him say, "Cool it, Matt." Wyndham swiveled around on his stool, spotted me, and said, "Ock."

"Hello, Mr. Wyndham," I said.

"Ah — who — how did you get in here?"

"Well, it only costs forty-five-hundred dollars — "

"Are you a member?"

"Not really. Actually, I sneaked in. Security is lax. Which is one of the things I want to talk to you about." I looked at the other man and said deliberately, "How do you do?"

His eyes shifted to Wyndham's pink-cheeked face and he said softly, "See you later, Matt."

I grabbed his right hand and pumped it while smiling and saying, "How do you do, sir? Any friend of Matt's . . . " I just let it trail off. So did he.

He had a pale, thin face, not unhandsome but a bit weak, I thought, with widely spaced blue eyes, a hairline mustache splitting his upper lip, and something like axle grease holding his black hair in tortured waves. He did not smile back at me, and it was clear he wasn't about to introduce himself.

But Wyndham, a bit flustered, said, "Oh, pardon me. Mr. Scott, this is Dr. Noble, Dr. Fleming Noble. Doctor, this is Mr. Sheldon Scott."

"A doctor, hey?" I said. I let go of his hand. "Well, I can't know too many doctors. Any day now I may call on you to have a bullet removed from my head."

Stiffly he said, "I wouldn't be of much help, in that case, Mr. Scott." He hesitated, glanced at Wyndham, then said easily, "I am a gynecologist. So we probably won't see each other again."

"Maybe not. Well, nice meeting you, doctor."

He walked away without even saying it was nice meeting me too. Wyndham reached for a highball on the bar and lowered its level by a couple of fingers. Then he looked at me, showed me his neat white teeth in a neat white smile, and said, "Well, ah, I'm rather surprised to see you here, Mr. Scott."

"I thought maybe you would be." The two stools next to us were empty, so we could talk quietly without being overheard.

"Are you a guest, or — "

"No, I came here to see you," I said. "First, though, to fulfill an obligation, I have a message from your wife. She wants you to return to the table immediately. Now, let's talk about a guy named Foster."

"Foster?" He blinked, moistened his lips, glanced at his wife's table, sighed, and said again, "Foster?"

"You know who I mean, don't you?"

"Well, I'm not . . . there was a gentleman in my office this afternoon, before you came in . . ."

"That's the cat. I just killed him."

His fleshy pink face didn't look quite so pink. I wouldn't say he paled, just got less pink. "My goodness," he said. He didn't seem greatly surprised at the news, but it was clear he wasn't enjoying this moment. I didn't want him to enjoy it.

"Here's a little background," I said, "so you can get the picture. Before I called on you I went to see a man named Eddy Sly. When I saw Eddy again, later, this Foster and another guy were with him. In fact, they were beating hell out of him. Now, the fact that they knew I'd seen Eddy means — unless they were watching Eddy's place, which isn't at all likely — that they had bees tailing me."

"I don't see what this has to do with me."

"I'll get to that now, Mr. Wyndham. After seeing Eddy Sly, I went to Universal Electronics, and your office. Out of your office, in a great rush, came Foster. He swallowed his gum when he saw me, then zipped out. A little bit later I saw him in a nearby bar, and the next time I saw him, I shot him. Because he was about to shoot me, Mr. Wyndham. When guys try to knock me off and I am forced to kill them, I get interested in their backgrounds and previous movements. His previous movements included a visit to you in your office. Did *he* tell you I was a detective? I didn't, you know." I paused, let him consider that, and went on pleasantly, "I'm sure you won't mind if I ask what his business was with you, Mr. Wyndham."

"Why . . . this is all most astonishing. He represents — or said he represented — the Victor-Cony Company, which makes transistorized radios and compact television receivers. The company is interested in a miniaturized power pack we've developed, and was considering the purchase of several thousand units. At least that is what he told me."

"If he said that, I'll bet he lied. Earlier today you told me you didn't know a man named Axel Scalzo. You want to tell me again that you don't know him?"

"Scalzo? I do not know anyone of that name, as I did indeed tell you before, Mr. Scott." A bit of indignation edged into his deep, rich voice. "Are you suggesting — "

"I'm not suggesting anything yet, Mr. Wyndham. I merely proffer facts for your consideration. The next of which is that when Poster yanked out a gun and pointed it at me, the other chap I mentioned was blazing at me with a large pistol. We both missed each other, in a remarkable display of poor marksmanship, so he got away. But he is alleged to be an associate or intimate of Axel Scalzo. And he was certainly thick as thieves with Foster, your alleged representative of Victor-Cony Company."

"So?" Wyndham stared at me. "This fact is perhaps remarkable, but it can, and does, have no significance to me. I've told you what my knowledge of Mr. Foster is. I have no knowledge whatever of this other person or your Mr. Scalzo." He raised an eyebrow. "And I confess to a growing curiosity. Why are you telling me all this?"

"I'm merely seeking to learn more about the late Mr. Foster, and his friends. Incidentally, this Dr. Noble — does he have an office in town?"

"Yes, in the Western Insurance Building."

"And he's a gynecologist." I grinned. "Then he can hardly be your personal physician, can he?"

"No, he . . . was of assistance to my wife a year or two ago. But that is truly no concern of yours, Mr. Scott."

"Certainly not. Except that your wife told me she'd never seen the man before."

He blinked, and slowly moistened his lips again. "How very strange," he said. "She must have forgotten. She . . . hasn't been well."

She looked strong as an ox to me, but I didn't mention that to Mr. Wyndham.

He stood up. "I really must return to my wi — my table, Mr. Scott. If you have no further questions . . ."

"That's it, I guess. Thanks for the time."

He took a couple steps toward his table and I said, "There is one thing. Can you tell me anything about Ardis Ames?"

His knees actually buckled. He stumbled, caught his balance. I hadn't expected much of a reaction; I'd just tossed the name at him because Foster and friend had quizzed Eddy Sly about a woman of that name.

But Wyndham stood stiffly a yard from me for long moments. "What?" he said.

Then he turned to face me. "Who?"

"Ardis Ames."

"Who is Ardis Ames?"

"Search me," I said. "Don't you know?"

He shook his head. "I have no idea."

Then he turned and walked to his table and joined Mrs. Wyndham. She started giving him hell. He didn't appear to be listening. Maybe it was just his way when Mrs. Wyndham was giving him hell. But his face was hardly pink at all now; in fact, he was definitely pale.

Well, I thought, for a shot in the dark I'd sure hit a nerve that time. But what had I hit it with? Who was this Ardis Ames? Who — or what?

I didn't know. But this I knew: Matthew Wyndham was a liar.

As I walked out of the Beverly Club I kept my eyes peeled and spotted Dr. Fleming Noble having a beer at the other end of the long bar. I nodded to him as I passed, but he seemed not to see me.

I got my Cad from the attendant, then drove back into the lot, thirty yards or so from the entrance, parked and waited. Ten minutes later Dr. Noble came out. The attendant trotted into the lot and drove a new Buick Electra up to the entrance. The doctor climbed into it and drove toward Beverly Boulevard.

I let him get a block ahead before I swung in after him.

Eight

I had no difficulty trailing the Electra down Beverly to the Angeles-Sands Hotel, half a mile away. Dr. Noble left his car in front of the hotel, spoke to the doorman, then went on inside.

By the time I'd parked and trotted into the hotel lobby, Noble was out of sight. I took a step toward the desk — then stopped. Noble had just appeared on my right, coming through an arched doorway above which red letters spelled out the name Unicorn Lounge, apparently the bar. He was with a blonde gal, who, fortunately, was occupying all his attention — fortunately, because I didn't want the guy to see me at the moment. Considering the gal, it was understandable that he didn't look my way.

She was almost enough to stop traffic on the Freeway, and for one nerve-twanging moment I thought it was Doody, but that was mainly because of the traffic-stopping figure — that and the blond hair. It jarred me until I noted that her face, though quite pretty, was older and harder than Doody's, the hair lighter, and she was at least two or three inches taller.

I didn't spend much time examining all that, however, because I was moving back toward the hotel entrance, edging behind an ersatz-marble pillar at the left of the door. Noble walked the blonde to the elevator and stood there a moment talking to her, caressing his hairline mustache with a dashing knuckle, then laughed at something and patted her generous fanny — generous to him, anyway — as she stepped into the elevator.

He walked to the newsstand and bought a pack of cigarettes. Squinting, I saw the elevator needle move up to "3" and stop. Noble turned and came straight toward the hotel entrance. Toward the entrance — and me. If he spotted me I was going to have to do some very speedy thinking to explain why I was hiding here behind a pillar, but he walked on past and out the door without a glance in my direction. I waited until he'd climbed into his Buick and pulled away from the curb before I hurried out after him.

Noble not only got a good head start on me, but drove faster than the law allows, and I almost lost him. But I kept getting glimpses of the Electra as he wove in and out of traffic, heading toward downtown Hollywood. He wasn't far ahead of me when we reached Sunset, but I missed the light. When it changed I gunned the Cad and narrowed the distance between us again, then suddenly he pulled over to the curb. I kept on going, slowing slightly. He was parked in front of a small apartment building, and I heard his horn blast a couple of times. As I drove past I caught a quick glimpse of a woman running down the cement walk toward his car. So he'd been sitting there honking for his date, huh? The clod.

She was another blonde, a blur of white — white dress or coat topped by light hair. As I turned right at the next corner she was slipping into the car. Probably had to open the door herself, I thought, since he not only sat there and honked, but was one of those guys with a hairline mustache. I turned around in a driveway and was headed back toward Sunset as the Electra turned left off the Boulevard.

This time he was easy to follow; left again to Vine, right to Beverly, left again and past the Beverly Club. When we were a block from the Angeles-Sands I began wondering if that was where we were all going. Maybe he was collecting blondes. But no, we went by the hotel and on to Third Street. And then, with a queer hair-prickling premonition, I knew where we were going. And I was right. The Electra pulled into the lot behind the South Seas.

Until this moment I'd had no overwhelmingly logical reason for following Dr. Noble, but the chase had been based on more than merely a whim since he'd been talking to Matthew Wyndham, and I was becoming increasingly curious about people chummy with Wyndham.

Now, though, I could feel the beginning of mild tension in my body. Maybe Noble and his gal were simply thirsty, and had stopped at a handy booze parlor for a drink. But maybe some previously loose threads were tightening into a knot.

I parked the Cadillac, smoked a cigarette, then took a few slow deep breaths to recharge my corpuscles, and went into the South Seas.

Even before I went through the front doors I could hear the bounce and belt of jazzy music from inside the club. Or maybe jazzy wasn't the word. It was pulsing, solid, with a heavy beat, almost like the music you hear . . . Yeah.

This, after all, was Amateur Strip Night at the South Seas. And the music was charged with the hot-and-heavy bounce, the draggy suggestive beat, of that music to which tomatoes peel, to which bountiful ladies move about while undressing in public. You may as well know the truth — I have very little objection to bountiful ladies undressing in public. In fact, I have even less objection to their undressing in private. Of course, this is frowned on in some quarters, I know; but hell, even drinking goat's milk is frowned on in some quarters, and when it comes to sex . . .

Well, sex. It's a funny thing: here in the U. S. of A. s-e-x is like the purloined letter in reverse — we know it's right there in plain sight, but pretend not to see it. Everywhere you look: boing — something sexy. Movies, books, magazines, Madison Avenue, billboards, television commercials — wow, television. In two hours of twisting the dial you can see more nude and seminude tomatoes, and even potatoes, showering, tubbing, rubbing, shampooing, wiggling, smelling, smoking, puckering, and doing practically every ring-a-ding "ing" you can think of, and for what purpose? What else? To get raped, of course. That is the only possible conclusion a balanced mind could draw from all this feverish preparation. A spot of this, two dabs of that, a spray or squirt or splash of the other and — go to black: we can't show it on television.

And remember, for Pete's sake, don't *do* anything sexy. Look sexy, feel sexy, smell sexy, act sexy, but don't *sex* sexy. That's the way it is in the U. S. of A., like a "how to" manual that says on the last page, "Now that you know how to do it, don't."

I took some more deep breaths, for my sexy corpuscles, and charged eagerly ahead.

The place was jammed. Every stool at the long bar on my left was being sat upon, every table I could see was occupied by at least two people. Beneath the music was a constant bubble and hum of conversation and laughter. There were guys in suits and sports outfits, women in cocktail gowns and print dresses and even a few wearing slacks or skin-tight Capris. The smells of liquor, perfumes, smoke mingled in my nostrils. A woman wearing a mink stole squeezed past me, the soft fur tickling my hand.

At first I didn't think I was going to find a seat. I walked toward the dance floor in the rear, keeping an eye peeled for Dr. Noble while hunting for a chair or stool. I hadn't seen Noble yet, but as I approached the piano bar a middle-aged man seated there glanced at his watch and let out a small squawk of surprise, then speedily left his stool and headed toward the door. He was in for it when he got home, I guessed.

I grabbed his seat at the piano bar and turned toward the action he'd been watching. I didn't know how long the show had been on, but the current performer had obviously been performing for more than a few seconds, and I could understand why the middle-aged guy might have stayed out longer than he'd intended.

At center stage, her body bathed by the glow from a rosy spotlight, a little black-haired gal was in a conniption of activity. She wore, from the floor up, high-heeled black shoes, black pants fringed with lace, a low-cut black brassiere, and an expression of huge satisfaction, and she was gyrating in what appeared to be a blend of old-time Charleston and any-old-time abandon. From her smiling lips came a high keening sound, as of large hinges squeaking, and just when it appeared the black brassiere was going to be propelled into orbit, the band hit a loud chord and held it.

And held it.

And held it.

Finally the little black-haired gal got the message. She stopped suddenly, then clapped her hands delightedly and jumped up and down. There was a great deal of applause.

I stopped applauding and ordered a drink from a bosomy waitress in a blue cleavage-necked blouse and blue V-sided shorts and black net stockings, as a slick-haired male M.C. stepped to stage center holding a small microphone near his rosy lips and cried:

"How about that? Hey, how *about* that? Well, folks, that was Mabel, our second amateur contestant of the night — and we've got four more to go. Remember, your applause picks the winner, the little lady who wins the fifty dollars and a screen test from Apex Productions."

Apex Productions. I had never heard of Apex Productions. Probably it consisted of the bar owner and a home-movie camera.

Then I remembered the bar owner was Axel Scalzo. And suddenly, with something like a double shock, I saw him. Double.shock because he was seated at ringside, on the right edge of the dance floor, sharing a table with the tall, thin, hairline-mustached clod, Dr. Noble.

At another table — right behind Scalzo, naturally — sat two hard-faced musclemen. One of them I knew quite well; too well. He was a tall, wide man with a flat face, a face that had been pounded much in the days when he'd been a pro boxer, and on numerous occasions since then — including a couple of times by me. He was the joker who had joyfully kicked in two of my ribs, and who now walked with a permanent limp. His name was Hale, and these days, wherever Scalzo went, there went Hale. The other man was a mug named Deke whom I'd seen with Scalzo a time or two, nearly as tall as Hale but thinner, a mean-looking hood with eyes cold and black as the edge of space.

Scalzo and Dr. Noble were at their table alone; the blonde wasn't with them. I hadn't even begun wondering where she might be, since I was still busy considering the pregnant possibilities inherent in the chumminess of Scalzo and Noble, when the M.C.'s voice filtered into my thoughts:

". . . applause decides the winner, so let's hear it for number three now, let's hear it for — Nell."

Nell? That was funny, I thought. Two Nells in one afternoon. Would wonders never cease?

Scalzo and Dr. Noble were beating their hands together with great vigor, Scalzo's shiny-bald scalp gleaming in the dim light as he bobbed his head. Dr. Noble was grinning widely. I looked away from them as the spotlight changed from pinkish to pale blue and the hand swung into an oldie, "Diane."

The next gal was gliding onstage now, moving with slow, sensuous grace, and it was suddenly less noisy in the club. Something in the way this one came on, or moved, or looked, reached out into the smoke-filled room and grabbed attention, held it. Slowly it became quiet.

She was about five-five or five-six, with a shockingly shapely body covered from throat to knees by a white dress that caressed every curve, hugged each protrusion and undulation. Her thick blond hair, almost silver in the blue light, hung loose and brushed her shoulders as she moved over the floor.

She spun, glided, then stopped momentarily facing the table at which Scalzo and Noble sat, arms lifting to raise the thick hair and let it fall heavily about her shoulders.

Then she turned, smiling slightly, and I knew that smile. I knew that face, that form, the thick hair that wasn't really silvery but rust-blond hair, the color of falling leaves in autumn.

It couldn't be.

The hell it couldn't.

In the silence, until then broken only by the subdued music, there was one explosive sound. I made it. It popped from my lips, flew forth from my gaping chips.

"*Doody!*"

Nine

She missed a step.

She — Doody, Nell Duden, my dopey Doody.

Some heads turned toward me. Not many. Enough. Hers, of course. And Axel Scalzo's. And Dr. Noble's. Hale and Deke stood up, stared, then slowly sat down. There were others, but it was those four male eyes from the ringside table that lit on me like the bores of four .45's.

The two men looked at each other then, and finally turned their attention toward Doody again. So did I. I sure as hell couldn't fade away into the crowd now. I hadn't really intended to in the first place; but even if I'd wanted to, I sure couldn't do it now.

Doody missed that one step but quickly recovered, caught the beat of the music again. For several seconds she swayed from side to side slowly, looking at me in a continuation of her initial surprise — or shock, pleasure, depression, whatever it was. Then she jerked her head, rope of hair whipping, and moved into her dance.

Well, friends, there were still three to go, but everybody in that hushed room knew who the winner was before another minute passed. This was rhythm, grace, beauty, and all of it wrapped in an aura of pulsing passion hot enough to scorch your eyeballs — yet there wasn't a movement, a sway, an arch of waist or thrust of hips that anyone, even blue-nosed reformers or professional censors, could in honesty have called crude or vulgar or obscene. It was simply — there's that word again — sexy as hell.

She stripped, as had the previous girl, to brassiere and panties and high-heeled shoes, one difference being that her wispy brassiere and step-ins were white and the shoes were white, another that her movements were slow, studied, smooth.

But the big difference was that this was Doody, and the dance was pure, packed, unadulterated sex. Sex charged with joy and free of shame, the chaste offering of an aphrodisiacally curved body, bulge of white breasts and mound of rounded hip, gleam of firm thigh moving erotically in the blue illumination. The light dimmed even more and seemed to strip her body bare. She moved, clothed but suddenly appearing unclothed, like a nude wraith or phantasm of blue smoke, as the tempo of the music increased, throbbing hotly, like a heart beating faster and faster. Her hair fell to cover her face, only to be brushed aside by her hands in a slow caress that was like the parting of a veil.

And then she stopped, rose on tiptoe with her cupped hands reaching high above her head, body arched, taut and unmoving, flesh gleaming faintly like a blue marble statue in moonlight. The music ended. The dim spotlight winked out. Still the silence remained. The house lights came up slowly. Doody was gone.

The M.C. appeared and cried jovially, "How about that? Hey, how *about* that?"

Then — the applause. A roar, a boom, a sea of sound, beating, pounding, whistling, and whooping. I started to finish my drink and discovered that, sometime in the last two or three minutes, I had finished it and one ice cube. So I ordered another as the M.C. continued his patter.

The girls entered from the left for their acts, and now through the drapes on the right came Doody, fully dressed in white again, and appearing even more lovely than when I'd first seen her at Universal Electronics. She walked — naturally — to the table at which sat Dr. Noble and Axel Scalzo.

Another dancer, this time a gal named Loris, was introduced and began her amateur strip, but I didn't look. She could have taken everything off and danced on the tables, and it would still have been an anticlimax. Not only did it seem to me there was little else to see after what I'd just seen, but while watching Doody I had not even thought about thinking. Now, though, while I sipped the drink, I wondered.

What in hell is going on here? I wondered.

A heavy hand fell on my shoulder. It is one of my idiosyncrasies that I enjoy few things in life less than heavy hands clopping my shoulders. Or banging me in the back, even pleasantly, or stiff fingers poking at me and such. I simply do not like guys laying bands on me, even in high good fellowship.

So I was starting to steam a bit even before I wheeled around to look at the hard, pursed-mouthed, not-charming face and shiny-bald head of Axel Scalzo. Behind him were Hale and Deke.

"Beat it, Scott," Scalzo said softly.

He had already removed his hand and now both fists rested on his hips. He stood with his legs slightly apart, looking down at me. Down at me because, though he was a couple of inches under my six-two, I was seated on a bar stool.

So I stood up, looked down at him instead, and said, "Scalzo, if you lay a hand on me again you'd better make it a fist."

"Knock off the big-mouth, Scott. Beat it. Take a walk."

I had a pull at my drink, using the time to calm myself down a little. Then I said, "No, thanks. I enjoy watching the gals dance. It's a public place, I'm quiet, peaceable — " "Peaceable." He laughed.

"Yeah, peaceable — so far. Keep pushing and you'll change all that, but peaceable so far, Scalzo. You'd pay hell calling the law to kick me out. And the only alternative is to throw me out." I grinned past him at Hale and Deke. "Hello, Hale," I said. "Stomped any ribs in lately?"

If anything, his sleepy-looking eyes got even more heavy-lidded, but he didn't speak. Deke could have been measuring me for a coffin.

Scalzo glared at me. He opened his mouth, and instead of drool, his soft, gentle voice came out saying, "That's the way you want it, O.K. I got no beef with you right now, Scott. Not right now. I just can't stand your goddamn guts. But O.K., you want to stay — and you don't cause no trouble — I won't push it. Just don't cause me no *trouble*."

"That depends," I said.

"On what?"

"You, Scalzo."

He chewed on the inside of his lip, looking levelly at me from the large gray eyes under the pinkish brows. The band was playing something hot and heavy, and on the floor Loris was squealing, either in pain or approaching ecstasy. Somebody near me coughed with a honk.

"What's that mean?" Scalzo asked softly.

"Well, when you sent your boys to work over Sick Eddy Sly — "

"Wait a minute." He scowled. "What the hell you pulling off, Scott? I know Sick Eddy, sure, who don't? I'm surprised he ain't here tonight." He paused, still scowling, and then continued, "But I never sent no boys to work him over. Who says I did?"

"Me. The muscle guys were a hood named Foster, and another joker known to hang around with you and your boys."

"I don't even know any Foster. Foster what — or what Foster? And who's this other guy?"

"Frankly, I don't know what Foster, or the other man's name is. Not yet. Foster is now dead, anyway — we were trying to shoot each other, and he didn't try hard enough — but the other mug is reputed to be one of your buddies." I described the guy but Scalzo just kept shaking his head.

"Whoever reputed it is full of fertilizer," he said, not saying fertilizer at all, actually. "He's nobody mixed up with me."

"Maybe not. Just one other thing, then. I find it curiously interesting that Dr. Noble over there, who was jawing with Matthew Wyndham very soon after I shot Foster and chased off his chum — neither of whom you ever heard of, of course — should then race here to the South Seas for further dialogue with Axel Scalzo."

"Who in hell is Matthew Wyndham?"

"Don't tell me you never heard of the president of Universal Electronics. I know damned well you've bought a hunk of UE stock."

"Sure, I got UE. I also got GM, AT and T, Packard-Bell, Sperry Rand — Why should it bug *you?*" He paused. "Yeah, Wyndham, now I know who you mean. But I don't know *him*. Never met him and got no reason to." He shook his head. "Scott, have another drink and get the hell out of here."

"Uh-huh. And you didn't know that the gal with Noble is Wyndham's secretary?"

He blinked slowly three times. "You're kidding."

I didn't say anything.

"What do you know? Who'd think a damned secretary . . ." Scalzo let it trail off, glancing across the room at Doody. "I figured she must be a ringer, a professional stripper rung in on me. The doc, now, him I know. That's why I joined him at the table — him and the babe. But the rest of it? You're full of fertilizer."

He shrugged and walked away, followed by his silent buddies. I didn't try to stop him. Either he was lying very convincingly — no

69

great trick for Scalzo, since lying was second nature to him — or I was in the wrong ball park.

I finished my drink, then slid off my stool and headed for the table where Doody, Noble, and now Scalzo were sitting. Except in special situations I make an effort to stay out of places where I'm not wanted, and I'm not much of a table-hopper, but this was a special situation. So I table-hopped.

When I stopped next to their table Scalzo half rose from his seat. "Scott, I told you — "

"Oh, relax, Scalzo. Just wanted to say hello to your friends." I grinned down at Doody and said, "Hello."

"Shellie," she said brightly. "What did you mean yelling at me like that? I almost jumped out of my skin . . . I mean, out of . . . well, I sure jumped."

"Yeah. The truth is, Doody, it wasn't exactly a yell, but more of an involuntary screech, or whoop, or . . . forget it."

"It sure was that, all right."

Scalzo finally sat back down in his chair, looking as if somebody had slipped an egg under him. Dr. Noble had pretty much the same expression on his thin, pale face. I said to him, "This is a coincidence, isn't it, doctor?"

"Isn't it?" he said flatly. He glanced up, looking as if he'd like to operate on me with a switchblade scalpel, then flicked his eyes away.

"I didn't know you were acquainted with Dr. Noble and Scalzo," I said to Doody.

"I came here with Dr. Noble," she said. "We met when he came to see Mr. Wyndham. But I've just this minute, practically, met Mr. Scalzo." She batted her big beige eyes across the table at him. "You know, he's the *owner* of this place, and he's even the owner of Apex Productions too. And do you know what? I get a — "

"Screen test." I finished it for her. "Apex Productions," I said, grinning at Scalzo. "Eight-millimeter epics in narrow screen and dying color, the apex of nadirs — "

"Scott — " Scalzo started to say something, then chopped it off. His face flushed, color rising clear up into his scalp. A vein I hadn't noticed before appeared in the exact center of his forehead. He looked past me, at the far wall — or maybe at the new dancer now bouncing about on the floor. But he wasn't seeing her, or the wall, and there was murder in his pale-gray eyes.

"You were wonderful out there," I said to Doody, nodding toward the dance floor. "I mean it. Marvelous, splendid — "

"It was *fun*," she interrupted me excitedly. "I never did anything like that before, but it was — oh, I got all goose-bumply. I was just telling Fleming — Dr. Noble, I mean — and Mr. Scalzo, I was simply perilized before my turn to do it, but as soon as I started getting started I wasn't perilized. Once was enough, though. It's like they say, if at first you succeed don't try it again and again . . . or whatever it is. I'm glad I did it, though."

"So, I'll wager, is everybody else. I know *I* wouldn't have missed — "

I cut it off. Movement at the drapes behind and to the right of the stage caught my eye and I glanced up, seeing a face that froze the words in my throat. Black eyes and brows, thin nose, thick lips and a scar on that upper lip. Foster's co-muscleman. The s.o.b. who'd pounded on Eddy — and shot me in the rear end.

He had started into the room, but he spotted me then and his eyes widened suddenly. I started around the table after him and he jumped back through the drapes and out of sight. I wasn't thinking about a thing except getting my hands on that bastard, and as I went past Scalzo's chair I hardly noticed as he reached out and grabbed my coat.

But it slowed me, yanked me around. I didn't hesitate. I slammed the edge of my hand into the side of Scalzo's thick neck and he let out a sharp, clotted sound. His grip loosened. I pulled free and ran through the draped archway. Backstage there was clutter and confusion, boxes piled against a wall, naked lights hanging from the bare ceiling. On my left a girl in a dark skirt and pink brassiere was holding a blouse in both hands, looking to my right. She swung her head toward me as I heard the pounding of feet and then the slamming of a door — to my right, where she'd been staring.

I ran that way, along a short narrow hall to a door slightly ajar, yanked it open and leaped through — and *blam*.

It was like getting stepped on by an elephant.

Ten

I went down, rolling, hanging onto consciousness but with pain caroming inside my skull, dots of light and bright jagged flashes growing and crumpling behind my eyes. But I had enough sense, or instinct, to keep rolling, grabbing under my coat for the .38.

Then I was on my side, moving my legs but not quite coordinated enough to get them under me in that first second. When I did get to my knees, then onto my feet, swaying, I heard the fading sound of shoe leather on pavement. He'd waited outside the door to slam me if I came through, but he hadn't waited around after that. He must have been a block away by the time I got started, and it took me a little while to get up any real speed. I didn't have a chance to catch him.

I leaned against the side of a car parked on a street intersecting Third. I couldn't even hear the running feet any longer. And my head felt like Ruin. I stayed against the car, found cigarettes in my pocket, and had a smoke, then walked slowly back toward the South Seas.

Toward it. I didn't intend to go back in it; that failed to impress me as a clever thing to do at the moment. Scalzo, let it be instantly understood, took no more joy than did I in being pawed by people, even in friendly fashion. And that hadn't exactly been a friendly dig I'd given him.

A trickle of warm blood ran down the back of my neck and I blotted it with a handkerchief, dabbed at my sore scalp. I made it to the Cadillac before anybody had time to wire bombs under the hood, and I didn't see anyone nearby who looked menacing. So I got in, did not blow up, and drove away from the club.

I knocked at Eddy Sly's door, went inside when he opened it.

Two fingers were in splints and a white patch loomed over one bloodshot eye, but otherwise he looked normal. Which is to say, on the verge of collapse.

He blinked through the bifocals at me. "What brings you back?"

"I've got a check in my pocket to cover, at least in part, services rendered so far." I slipped the check from my wallet and handed it to him. "And there's one more job for you, Eddy, if you feel up to it."

He looked at the check, scratched his thin black hair, raised his eyebrows, lowered them. "Well, I don't really feel up to it," he said. He looked at the check again. "But I feel better than I did. What's the job?"

"Simple enough. I want you to tag a guy for me if you can. If you can't make him, O.K., I'll try another way."

"Just so I don't have to get shot or strangled or anything unnecessary like that."

"We won't let it happen unless it's essential."

"You're fun," he said.

Eddy and I went down to the lobby where I put in a call to the Spartan Apartment Hotel, which I call home, and got Dr. Paul Anson.

"Hi, Paul," I said. "Shell. I've got a medical question. Your usual fee?"

"Indeed. Three Martinis. Shoot."

"What kind of doctor is a gynecologist? I know roughly, but give me the sharp picture."

"Well, first of all you mispronounced it, you imbecile. You might find it your way in dictionaries, but among gynecologists themselves — sometimes gynies, familiarly, as among nurses — it's pronounced with a hard *g* and to rhyme with wine, not gyne, as in gyne-and-vermouth. That will be three Martinis, very light on the gyne."

"Try for six."

"A gynecologist, who is usually also an obstetrician — hence our unpronounceable abbreviation for them: obgyn — is a physician and often surgeon who specializes in the treatment of women and their diseases, their hygiene, the weird and baffling and at times wholly imaginary afflictions to which the fair sex is heir, and they are very heiry when it comes to weird and baffling — "

"Oh, shut up."

But he told me anyway. More, much more, than I had ever hoped to know. "Fine," I said. "Fine; shut up! Look, I owe you a whole damned case of Martinis, O.K.?"

"That's the spirits. I knew psychology would work. But let me tell you one more little thing, which will simply ruin your life — "

I hung up on him.

We sat, Sick Eddy and I, in my Cadillac, at a spot from which we could watch the South Seas parking lot. I hadn't been back inside the place, but Dr. Noble's car was still there, so apparently he was still inside the club. I'd checked the registration slip in the Electra and it was made out to Fleming Noble, M.D., with a San Francisco address. Eddy sat on my right, holding a pair of my binoculars.

About forty minutes after we'd taken up our position I saw them come out and walk toward the Electra — Doody first, followed by the tall, thin cat with the negligible mustache.

"There they are," I said. "Get with it, Eddy."

He was already peering through the binoculars. "Easy," he said.

"That's the guy I want," I told him. "Dr. Noble."

"Dr. Noble, hell. That is Dandy Dan Quick."

I grinned. "It figured. I kind of thought a gynecologist would know how to pronounce it. Now, Eddy, how thick is Dandy Dan with Scalzo?"

"Very thin. No connection I know of."

"You're sure?"

"Dandy's been around Southern Cal a handful of years but I never heard of him messing with Scalzo. They're different types, different kind of work. Could be. Maybe I just never heard nothing."

"Yeah. Well, he and Scalzo are at least acquainted. And they've known each other for some time. Unless . . . somebody's conning me." I glanced over at the Buick Electra again. "Incidentally, I don't suppose you know the gal with Dandy, do you?"

"No, but I wouldn't mind. If I was healthier, that is. She's almost too much for my constitution even from this distance. But that's the kind he always uses."

"Uses? Uses how?"

"Dandy's one of the slickest con men this side of the slammer, but he's a highly horny papa besides, and usually works grifts like twists on the badger game, or a knock-up con, or maybe a little polite blackmail if the mark writes suitable letters to Dandy's roper — which is always a choice-looking bezark like that blonde there. Dandy could make it very large working the big con with top men, but he likes it his way, since like I said he is a highly horny papa. Plenty good men he could team up with, but he just don't like working with men."

Dandy Dan Quick — Dr. Noble had driven out of the lot without, I was certain, spotting us. I started the Cad and pulled into the street after him.

"Tell me more about the grift, Eddy."

Most of it I knew, but he filled me in.

The con man is usually a consummate actor. He has to be because he plays many parts — doctor, lawyer, banker, stock broker, mining engineer, you name it. He gets your money by making you believe the unreal is real: that a race is fixed, say; that a stock is going up, when it isn't, because if only you knew, you dear, there isn't any stock; that all the yellow stuff he shows you from the Good Fortune Mine is gold, when it is realty yellow stuff. The con man is clever, convincing, well-informed, and through such dodges as the race and stock and gold and others he hypnotizes loaded people, and proceeds to unload them, often in such clever fashion that the mark never wakes up, never even knows he's been dozing.

The trick is to stick the hooks into him at first ever so gently; then a little more, a little more, a little more. At first the mark believes a little, then more, and finally conviction is absolute — just as intelligent people once were convinced that the earth was flat and if you looked over the edge and said oops you were gone. The trick is to start small and build big, acting the right part as you go along, playing on the mark's hopes — and fears — and then, at the psychological moment, move in for the painless kill.

Even though sometimes it isn't really painless for the mark, it's *never* painful for the con man. They feel no pain. They laugh and laugh and laugh, while they count your money. They're happy sonsofbitches. And don't say it couldn't happen to you.

A top-notch confidence artist is usually a lovely person on the surface, warm, charming, intelligent — but he's got the grift in his eyes and larceny in his heart, and he speaks novocained words that go in your ears and paralyze your noodles. Add a woman to that and, man, it's murder. The con man with the gentle touch can make you believe Disneyland is South Pasadena and you can buy it for ten bucks a month. Consequently, the good ones live very high — not on the hog, rather on prime beef, crêpes and caviar, and those little chickens called Malayan hens.

When I asked Eddy what he'd meant by the "knock-up con" he said, "Well, Dandy Dan works a lot of variations on the basic bilk. That one's when he has the bim roping for him locate the mark, and if the mark's ready they manage to find a sack somewhere and toss around in it for a spell. After a couple months or so she ups to the mark and starts calling him Daddy."

"Uh-huh. And the sucker is probably married and has seventeen children."

And a large bank account. From that point you can work it north, south, or up. Maybe a cash payment, maybe dough for an abortion, maybe checks every month — choose your pick. Once the mark gets the convincer, and has spontaneously emptied his bladder, he is usually ready for about anything. Then Dandy works an out-and-out squeeze sometimes. Like if the mark is hooked and writes the lady letters saying, 'I shall never forget those mad nights in the sack, which I shall always remember' — like that, Dandy sells them back by the paragraph. Hell, Scott, there's a hundred gimmicks, and Dandy Dan is a expert at all of them."

Dandy Dan was now on Sunset again, and I was a block behind. It looked as if he was taking Doody home. I kind of hoped that if he started in with her, he would trip on the sill and break his mustache.

A block before we reached the Lanai Apartments, where Doody had told me she lived, I turned off Sunset, U-turned, and then parked facing Sunset near the intersection. I sat there, impatiently watching Dandy's car. When he finally came back to the Electra, only half an hour had dragged by. But it was a long half hour.

I caught him in three blocks and it was a repeat of the earlier episode. He went straight to the Angeles-Sands. I double-parked, told Eddy to slide under the Cad's wheel. Dan was stepping into the elevator as I entered the lobby. I walked briskly to the stairs and up them in a hurry.

He was still in the third-floor hallway when I got up there. I watched him use a key and go into 308.

In the lobby again, I stopped at the desk and said to the clerk, "Say, I just saw a man I think I know going into room 308. Would that be Mr. Angstrom?"

He checked his cards and shook his head. "No . . . Quick, Daniel. Mr. and Mrs. Quick in 308."

"Mr. and Mrs. Quick? You're sure it isn't Angstrom?"

He smiled. He was sure. So was I. I thanked him and went out to the Cad.

When I left Eddy in his room at the Gable I gave him another check.

"You don't need to give me no more loot, Scott," he said, taking the check. He peeked at it and smiled. "Though it do help make up for the terrible risks we just took."

"Yeah, but you were very brave, Eddy. Seriously, friend, thanks. I think this was a profitable night."

"You and me both," he said.

I went to the door, amused by an idle thought. For at least an hour, Eddy hadn't told me how painfully he was dying. He hadn't even mentioned any new symptoms.

But just as I opened the door he said to me, with an intent look on his face, "Scott, I was thinking."

"Yeah?"

"What kind of doctor is that you were talking about? That gynero-cerus or whatever you said — the kind Dandy isn't."

"Gynecologist?"

"That's the baby. I was wondering, maybe I should get one to check my plumbing. I been having some queer rumblings and twinges — "

"Not," I said, laughing, "queer enough."

"What's so funny?"

I didn't tell him, but the thought helped cheer me on my way.

The Spartan Apartment Hotel is on North Rossmore in Hollywood, hard by the Wilshire Country Club. I went up to the second floor, down the hall to my rooms, and inside, turning on the small lamp just inside the door — the dim one that lets the fish get used to some illumination before I turn on the brighter overhead lights.

The fish are inside the door, on the left as you enter my living room-bedroom-kitchenette-and-bath — a guppy aquarium and a community tank containing *Panchax chaperi*, *Rasbora heteromorpha*, several neons, mollies, and swords, and a few other varieties, including one splendid cornflower-blue *Betta splendens*, a particular prize not only because of the huge anal fin and rippling caudal, but because I hatched him myself from a wee egg. Yes, folks, I'm his mother.

After feeding the fish and watching them dash and glitter for a minute or two, I beamed at Amelia, my colorful-as-guppies nude in her yard-square frame over the fake fireplace, then walked to the chocolate-brown divan, sat, and picked up the phone.

It was not much after 1 A.M., so I called a bar where I'm known and ordered three dozen Martinis, mixed and poured into a jug, the jug to be delivered tomorrow, with one olive, to Dr. Paul Anson.

Then I thought if it wasn't so late, and if it wasn't so likely I'd have a well-crammed day tomorrow, I'd make one more call. I'd call Carmen.

But I steeled myself, sighed, got up, showered, and went to bed.

Thoughts rolled and silently collided in my head.

When I remembered Doody dancing, her nude-but-not-nude body swirling like smoke in blue light, I thought about Carmen again. But I pushed her out of my mind. I'm made of stem stuff.

I rolled over, thinking. Man, if I didn't have such a big day coming up tomorrow. If it wasn't so late. Man. Waowoo. Woweewow.

Hell, I might get killed tomorrow.

I called Carmen.

Eleven

Came the dawn.

Like thunder.

Like an enemy, creeping up on me.

I opened my eyes, smacked my lips. "Bluh."

"Hey, Carmen," I said.

Boy, I felt *awful*.

My head hurt, my knees hurt from falling on them, my chin hurt, and I guess you know what else hurt. Hell, I'd been shot in it.

"Hey, Carmen." No answer. Maybe she was dead. That made sense, since I was dead. We had both died in the night. But it seemed I could feel something moving in me, like cold molasses. My blood. There was life in the old boy yet.

"Hey, *Carmen*."

I opened my eyes and rolled over. I couldn't see a damn thing. Yeah, she was dead, all right; they'd come in and hauled her away.

No, now I remembered. I remembered her leaving. Clearly, now, I could recall her saying, "*Caramba!* Ees that sonlight? Ai, Chihuahua, eet ees the son coming op! *Madre de Dios!* Shellscott, gardamn you, eet ees the *son* coming op!"

"What's coming op?"

"The son!"

"How do you spell that?"

Zip, thump, swish, clatter — and she was gone.

I was puzzled. If the sun had been coming up then, and was just coming up now, how long had I slept?

Great. I remembered closing my eyes for a minute. Next thing was the alarm ringing. Yeah, I'd had some sleep. About a minute. Nothing like springing out of bed full of that old zip, hey? I sat up on the edge of the bed, and slowly fell backward.

Well, now I knew how Eddy felt all the time. But there was no help for it. I had to get up. I made it. As I said before, I'm made of stern stuff. I got up on the edge of the bed again. Then I was on my feet. I was standing. There's nothing a man can't do if he puts his mind to it. That gar-damn Carmen, I thought. That miserable Carmen. Anger plopped in me. Fire flared in my loins. No, not in my loins. But new strength trickled into me somewhere. And I tottered forward bravely, into the bright new day.

When I'd parked next to Pete's and walked back down Broadway to the Hamilton Building, I spotted the guy just inside the entrance, studying the building register. It's one of those boards listing all the tenants and their room numbers, so constructed that with a minimum of effort the letters or numbers can be removed and new ones inserted. Like if I got killed at 2 P.M. today, by 2:05 the management could have my name off the board and another in its place. Which shows how gay I still was this morning.

This guy wasn't much over five feet tall, fat and about forty. He didn't even glance around as I walked in. And that struck me as a bit odd. I went up the stairs, looked back at him. He was still studying the board.

I went on up to my office. I sat behind my desk, pulled the Colt Special from under my coat, and held it out of sight below the desk's edge, muzzle pointing toward the door.

In half a minute the door opened and the little fat man came inside. He nodded at me, said, "Good morning," and stepped toward the desk, reaching casually toward the left inside pocket of his coat.

I raised my gun.

He stopped, corners of his mouth pulling down and his eyes narrowing till they were almost shut. Then he said, "Easy, Scott. Easy." He moved his hand slowly inside his coat and when it came out he was holding, not a gun, but a thin sheaf of green bills.

I kept the gun on him, let him hear the click as I thumbed back the hammer.

I still hadn't said a word, and he licked his plump lips but slowly stepped closer. Then he dropped the bills on my desk and with a careful finger pushed them toward me over its mahogany surface.

"Will you put that heat away?" he said. "It makes me nervous."

"It's supposed to. Come on, what do you want?"

"A friend of mine — and yours — says he knows you got to work to earn a living, and you're on a job. Well, this loot is so you won't have to work for a while. You can take a vacation."

"A kind old philanthropist, huh?"

"What's that?"

"In this case, a loser."

"I don't get you."

I eased the Colt's hammer down and put the gun away, then picked up the money. There were fifty one-hundred-dollar bills.

"Five G's, huh?"

"It's a living."

"Our friend must be interested in making sure I take a good long vacation."

"Well, he doesn't want you to get killed."

"Who is this friendly sonofabitch?"

He scowled a little, but said, "Don't be a jerk. I wouldn't know. I'm only a messenger boy."

He knew. But he wouldn't tell me unless I pulled off his ears or performed some equally painful operation on him, which I wasn't going to do. But maybe I could find out who'd sent him anyway.

I said, "There must have been ninety-nine guys who tried to buy me off at one time or another, and it's never worked yet. I thought the word would be around by now."

"There's always a first time."

"Wrong again."

"My friend would maybe up the ante. Maybe plenty. Don't kid me, everybody's got some kind of price — "

He stopped because I had spread the bills, then slowly torn them in half, which wasn't easy. I slipped the top C-note from the bills without his noticing, then stacked the rest in a fairly neat pack and tossed them across the desk top.

He stared at the bills, then at me. After a while he picked up the money, looked at it for several seconds, and finally shoved the wad into his coat pocket. He stood there a little longer, as if undecided what to do, then turned suddenly and went out.

Standing at the window overlooking Broadway, I saw him leave the building and walk past Pete's and into the parking lot there. In a minute he came out driving a year-old Ford.

I watched him drive down Broadway, then went back to my desk and got on the phone. First I called the police. There was nothing new on the murder of John Kay; no leads, no suspects, nothing. I talked to men in Homicide, R and I, and Missing Persons, and asked several questions about Julie Tangier. There had been no Missing Person report on her, no report of disappearance, accident, death — a zero, in fact, on Julie Tangier. I asked the same questions about Ardis Ames. Zero again. Nothing from Missing Persons, the morgue, Homicide; R and I, the Records and Identification Division, had nothing on her. It was the same story when I checked on Alice Brandt, Wyndham's former secretary.

I stayed on the phone a few minutes longer, hung up, and sat doodling on a scratch pad, thinking. Then I called Gabriel Rothstein and told him I was ready to make an initial report if he wanted it. He wanted it. In another minute I was on my way to his office.

"Hello," he boomed as I walked in. "Our stock is down an eighth. You've lost one hundred and twenty-five dollars."

"That's nice. I had to shoot a guy, I've been wounded in the rear end and socked on the head, and this morning I feel as if vampires had used me unkindly during my minute's sleep. Now I've lost one hundred and twenty-five dollars. Well, easy come, easy go."

He laughed, apparently thinking that was marvelous, and stood up behind his desk to shake my hand.

"What have you learned?" he asked.

"Not much, really. Or, rather, a lot of little things that aren't tied together yet. I've found no direct link between Scalzo and Wyndham, but there are several people who know both of them — a con man named Quick, posing as a doctor; Wyndham's new secretary, a beautiful dumb blonde named Nell Duden; a hoodlum or two, one of them the guy I shot last night. Both Scalzo and Wyndham deny knowing each other, and I think they're both lying but can't prove it. Not yet. No leads so far to Kay's killer. Incidentally, I think you're being watched — this building, anyway."

"Oh? What makes you think that?"

"A little while after I left here yesterday I went to see a man named Eddy Sly. A couple of musclemen knew I'd gone to see him. The odds are they knew because they saw me go to his hotel, which means they must have been on my tail before then. Almost surely they had no reason to tail me until I took this job. They had a pretty good idea of what I was checking on, so they must have picked me up here."

He nodded slowly, ran a big hand over his short black hair. The almost chill blue eyes under the black brows were fixed on my face.

"Another thing," I added. "When they were bouncing Eddy around they asked him if I was working for you. Apparently they didn't *know* I was, but had reason to believe I might be. Say I was seen coming into this building. Well, there are a lot of other offices in it and I just might have been going to one of the others."

"I see," he said. He pulled at his nose. "Your complete report. Start at the beginning."

I brought Rothstein up to date. Just the facts, without comment or interpretation.

When I finished, he said, "Interesting. I presume you are intrigued by the same elements which now intrigue me. The peculiar unavailability of Miss Tangier, and of Miss Alice Brandt, Mr. Wyndham's former secretary, and his new secretary's familiarity with many of our dramatis personae. And, too, the very recent death of Mr. Kay."

"And what about the mysterious Mr. Quick?" He paused. "I presume you have visited the Western Insurance Building to determine if he has an office there as Dr. Noble?"

"I'm going to do that when I leave here, but I'm pretty sure what I'll find."

"Your conclusions from all this?"

"In abeyance for the moment. I'm getting a picture, but it's still fuzzy. With luck I'll have more for you later today or tonight. Whatever's cooking should by now be at a boil. We've applied some extra heat, and the animals should be pretty well stirred up. At least one of them was concerned enough to try buying me off."

"Yes." He nodded again. "When you tore those bills in half, was that a mere exhibition of contempt or anger, mere theatrics?"

"No."

"I thought not"

"Nobody — whether it's Scalzo, Wyndham, or somebody else — is going to toss five thousand bucks into the ash can. So in the next few days, or possibly even today, those bills will be presented somewhere for redemption, perhaps deposited to an account if we're lucky. It depends on whether the owner thinks my act was something more than mere theatrics."

He reached for a phone on his desk, dialed a number, and spoke briefly to someone he called Harry. Then he hung up and turned back to me. "That was the president of a bank where I have a rather large account. He'll let me know if the bills are deposited or redeemed anywhere in this area."

"Good. I'll check with you later."

He smiled pleasantly. "Since you have refused his offer of money, what will the man — assuming it is a man — do now?"

"Whoever it is, he's worried. At least five G's worth. If it's merely a worried citizen, perhaps nothing more will happen. If it was Scalzo, he'll probably try to kill me."

"And that doesn't concern you?"

"Don't kid yourself. It concerns me plenty. Maybe I should have been more alert to the possibility of somebody following me yesterday, but it seemed too early in the case to be worrying about a tail. But that won't happen again."

"What do you intend to do next?"

"I've got a big agency checking on Universal Electronics personnel, and I told them this morning, by phone, to dig into the possible whereabouts of Julie Tangier and Alice Brandt as well. Also this Ardis Ames I mentioned. If they fail to come up with anything, I'll try that route myself — but it's the kind of thing that can take days of checking and legwork, time I can better spend on the people who *are* available now. For the same reason I haven't gone through the police mug books looking for the second man who was working Eddy Sly over, and who clobbered me last night. Even if he's got a record here, it might take all day to find his picture, and he may not be in the L.A.P.D. books at all, which would mean more time wasted. Right now I'll check the Western Insurance Building, then I'm going to have a talk with Murphy."

"He's the man with whom Mr. Kay was sitting at the race track?"

"Right. The police got nothing from him, but there's a chance they missed something. Not that they aren't thorough; they are. But the police don't know as much as I do about what Kay was working on, and Murphy just might know something without realizing its importance. After that, well, part will depend on what Scalzo and Wyndham and the others do from now on. And I've got enough already, I think, to squeeze Matthew Wyndham. I'm just going to play it by ear. Push a little here, pull a little there, see what develops."

"Do it your way, Mr. Scott. I don't care what methods you use. All I require is total and absolute success."

I grinned. "Suits me. It's my stock too, you know."

"Yes." He grinned back at me. "Down an eighth."

In the lobby of the Western Insurance Building I studied the register. There was, of course, no Fleming Noble or Dr. Noble listed. There were several doctors listed, however, and it would have been a simple trick to remove the name of one and insert, say, "Fleming Noble, M.D."

I took off and headed for the home of Mr. William Murphy. He lived on Pelham Avenue in West L.A., in a big white house fronted by recently mowed green lawn. I found him behind the house in a hammock slung between two Chinese elm trees with a can of beer and a racing form. He was a pleasant man nearing sixty, wearing rumpled slacks and a colorful sports shirt, and didn't mind my interrupting his search for a winner.

"Do me good to get my mind off it for a few minutes," he said. "Maybe my subconscious'll gimme a horse in the sixth." He rubbed faint stubble on his chin. "It's a tight one."

He went through his story again for me. There wasn't anything new, nothing I hadn't already been told by the police. "Only thing I noticed was he didn't bet on any of the races. I guessed he just liked to watch 'em run," Murphy said.

I spent another five minutes with him, but it wasn't any help, and it was with more than a little disappointment that I prepared to leave. "Well, thanks very much, Mr. Murphy." I grinned. "Hope your horses are all in the money today."

"You play the ponies, Mr. Scott?"

"When I can get to the track."

He handed me the form. "Who you like in the sixth?"

"Well," I said after a minute or so, "Sirocco looks pretty good. Came in second at a mile five days ago, made up two lengths in the stretch. Should be sharp if he runs today."

"Kind of like him myself. Last out was his first time in the money for a while, too. Might be a good price." He paused. "Usually I go to Hollypark alone, easier to concentrate when I'm by myself. But you seem to know your horses. If you're at the track today, I'd be glad to make an exception and have you join me."

It struck me. Not because he'd said I could join him, and the last man to join him had been Kay, but because he'd said he'd "make an exception." Something floated in my mind, just out of reach.

I said, "You're usually alone at the track? I mean, you prefer being alone?"

"Well, ordinarily." He grinned. "I'm pretty serious about the horses. Not that I bet real big, nothing like that. But I keep records of money won and lost, you know? So far I'm three hundred and eight dollars ahead for the season."

"Mr. Murphy, if you usually prefer being alone, how come you didn't mind John Kay's joining you? He didn't know beans about horses."

He was silent for a moment, then lifted his trousers leg. On his left foot was a built-up shoe with an almost two-inch heel. "Doesn't bother me," he said. "But being kind of handicapped myself, I guess I've got, oh, a little more understanding of other handicapped people. Or sympathy — empathy, is that what you call it?"

"Handicapped? What do you mean? Kay didn't have anything wrong with him."

Murphy blinked. "He was deaf. I'd call that — "

"Deaf? He could hear a gun cocked two blocks away."

"Well, if he wasn't deaf, I don't know why he'd be wearing one of those hearing-aid things in his ear."

But I did. Suddenly, and with a quick surge of energy in my body. There was only one reason why a man with perfect hearing — especially an investigator like John Kay — would have been wearing a "hearing-aid thing" in his ear.

Slowly I said, "Mr. Murphy, was he carrying anything? A box, brief case, attaché — "

"Why, yes, he did have a brief case, but — "

I thanked Murphy again and left so fast he must have thought something had bitten me. In a way, something had.

Twelve

I headed for Inglewood and Hollywood Park, but stopped on the way and put in a call to Gabriel Rothstein. An idea was starting to take form, and if perchance Rothstein had news for me, I wanted to know about it now.

He did have news for me. "I'm glad you called, Mr. Scott," he said. "I heard from Harry — my friend at the bank — not more than ten minutes ago. That money was deposited within the last half hour at the Security-First National Bank branch on Cañon Drive in Beverly Hills."

"Who deposited it? To what account?"

"It was turned in for credit to one of the accounts in the name of our friend Mr. Scalzo. Does that surprise you?"

"Not much."

"I don't know the name of the man who brought in the money, but he answers the description of the individual you told me about."

"Uh-huh. What does surprise me a little is that he didn't take the cash straight to Scalzo himself. He must have phoned and told him I'd turned down the offer. But the little man must *not* have told Scalzo about my bisecting the bills. It's eight to five Scalzo would have tumbled if he had."

"There was one rather odd circumstance," Rothstein continued. "The amount was not five thousand dollars, but only forty-nine hundred."

"Yeah," I said. "I kept one of the bills. Now that I know it came from Scalzo, I think I'll return the C-note to him."

Rothstein was silent for a few seconds. Then he said, "But won't that let Mr. Scalzo know you've learned he was behind the bribe attempt?"

"Sure. I want him to know. You want action, don't you?"

"Yes, of course, but . . ." A short silence again. "Isn't it possible that Mr. Scalzo might become violent?" It was one of the few times Rothstein's voice hadn't sounded like an overturning gravel truck. He sounded almost subdued.

"Not possible," I said. "Inevitable. Hell, after last night, the moment he spots me he's going to become frenzied."

"I really don't intend for you to get murdered, Mr. Scott."

"You and me both. Look, Scalzo's probably not in the jolliest mood of his life right now, but I'm going to increase his depression, if possible. Couple things I want to tell him. If I can shake the burn up enough, maybe I can shake something out of him."

"I hope you know what you're doing, Mr. Scott."

"So do I, Mr. Rothstein."

We hung up.

And I changed my mind and headed for the home of Axel Scalzo. It was on Hollyridge Drive, adjacent to Brush Canyon, on the outskirts of Hollywood. I'd seen the house before but had never been inside. It was a big brick-and-redwood place, and there was nothing humble about this home. Scalzo had poured a hundred thousand bucks or more into the house and grounds.

A cement driveway led off the street to a double garage in which were parked a new Cadillac sedan and a Lincoln Continental convertible. I pulled up behind them and walked over flagstone steps set in dark-green Korean grass to the front door. I rang the bell. Nothing happened. I rang again. Soft chimes once more inside the house, that was all. So I took a walk around the side of the house.

Maybe Scalzo — and no telling who else — was in back. Somebody was here, or else the guy owned three cars. There were enough trees around this joint to make a forest, plus a lot of green stuff, ferns and bushy shrubs and large-leaved tropicals. I was walking over more of the flagstones which ran parallel to the house, but a narrow dirt path led off to my right, and glancing that way I caught a glimpse of white.

So I walked over the dirt path to a small clearing, well protected by the planting around it but open to sunlight pouring in from overhead. Face down, on her bare stomach, a gal lay on a blanket in the middle of the clearing, and she was either dressed in less than the law allowed or the law had been changed since the last time I looked. I've always figured that law ought to be changed anyway.

She was a blonde, splendidly curvaceous, wearing a pink Bikini bottom, the top caught beneath her bosom, its strap untied to allow the smooth play of sun on her back. She heard me breathing or something, or maybe my feet coming to a sliding stop, and flipped over onto her back, propping herself up on her elbows. Man, bosom wasn't the word; those were big, trembling breasts, not-yet-sun-pinked but tipped with pink-like jutting exclamation points, and they sure got a couple exclamations out of me.

In the middle of my exclamations she said, "Who the hell are you?"

Leisurely she reached behind her and picked up the Bikini top, then put it in place. Not exactly, but close enough. It was the blonde I'd seen with Dan Quick in the Angeles-Sands Hotel last night. Mrs. Quick — or would it be Mrs. Noble? Maybe even something else by this time.

I said, "I'm not a peeking Tom, miss. Or peeping whatever . . . um. Ah, is it miss?"

In a voice chill enough to freeze alcohol in distant thermometers, she said, "Mrs."

That was all; there wasn't any more. And I could tell there wasn't going to be any more. "The truth is," I said, "I came here to see Scalzo. Axel. Nobody answered my ring, so I . . . Ah, Axel around?"

She was squinting up at me, forehead slightly wrinkled, but nothing else wrinkled, the Bikini top even less exactly in place. "He's in back, by the pool. Who — Ye gods! You're Shell Scott!"

"Yes, ma'am."

"Ye gods. Don't go back there . . ."

"Something I shouldn't see?"

"It's not that. He'll just . . . have a hemorrhage probably. You must be nuts, coming here. Out of your skull, psycho." She paused. "You're really going back there?"

"Yep."

"This I've got to see."

She rose smoothly to her feet, gave a little tug to her Bikini top, and another little tug to her Bikini bottom — neither of which did a bit of good — then padded after me as I walked back to the flagstone path and on to the rear of the house.

It looked almost another half acre back here. Surrounded by smooth white cement, was a forty-foot-long swimming pool. On the left was a stone barbecue pit, a massive natural-wood table near it. This side of the pool were two metal tables with red-and-white-striped umbrellas over them, canvas-backed chairs around them.

Scalzo was next to the pool, sitting under one of the striped umbrellas, hairy hand hiding a highball. He was in swim trunks, and honest to God he looked as if armed attendants should have been tossing him hunks of raw giraffe meat. He was built along the general lines of a cement mixer anyway, and seeing the jungle of hair all over him began to understand how come he was bald. For a guy to grow that much fur that fast his hairy metabolism must have sucked everything but his scalp right off his head and down through his brains and out every which way. He was really hairy.

He didn't see me for a few seconds as I walked toward him. But Hale did. Hale, Scalzo's shadow, the guy always protectively near Scalzo. My buddy. He was fully clothed, lying in a chaise longue a few feet beyond his boss.

Slowly Hale sat up, eying me, his mouth opening.

"Hello, Scalzo," I said cheerfully.

He swung his bald head around and fixed those pale-gray eyes on me. He didn't move or blink, just stared. Then he said, "Scott. You got your nerve, you miserable sonofabitch."

"I shall pop you into the pool, Axel. Watch your mouth."

For a while there I thought he was going to let out the battle honk of the bull moose and come at me. He stood up, filled his chest with air, balled his right hand into a fist, Muscles writhed over his forearm, biceps, and shoulder.

Then he relaxed the arm, but not the rest of him. "You could get killed," he said, "sneaking in here like this."

"I didn't sneak. Fact is, I rang the bell but there wasn't any answer. I came out here to give you something. Give something back, that is."

"Huh?" He was puzzled.

I took my wallet from my inside coat pocket — easily, and keeping an eye on Hale, who almost yanked out a gun and shot me anyway — and took the two halves of the torn hundred-dollar bill from my wallet. I handed them to Scalzo and he took them, an expression of great perplexity on his face. Which told me clearly enough that he didn't know anything about my tearing the bills in the first place.

So I told him the tale. "Your secret's out, Scalzo. I guess your messenger boy has to go stand in the corner."

"That dumb sonofabitch," he said. Then he looked at me and grinned. Not pleasantly, just grinned. "O.K., so what? You should of took the five G's, Scott. It would of been the easy way."

"What's the hard way?"

He took two long strides toward me, stopped a foot away. He glared up at me, and his voice was soft, level, and very cold indeed. "Why, you get yourself killed, you sonofabitch."

I felt my hand jerk. I balled it into a fist, but managed to hold the hand at my side. I did not intend to get shot in the head — or, for that matter, to shoot anybody else in the head — unless it became absolutely necessary. I could feel the tightness spread from my arm into my back muscles, slowly down into my thighs.

"The mouth," I said finally. "I told you, I shall pop you into the pool."

He laughed. "Well, I can wait. You aren't gonna last, Scott."

"You've got it backward. I've got you pegged now, Scalzo. You're shook up enough so you tried to buy me off, and now you know I know it." I grinned at him. "That's all I needed; that ties you in, Scalzo. So I'm going to ruin you, and whatever crooked caper you're pulling. I'm going to put a bug in Wyndham's ear — about Dr. Quick, for one thing. I know most of it already and I'll have the rest in a matter of hours. Enough. Enough to put the chill on you, Scalzo."

He swallowed, as if startled. "Sure. We'll see. And I still owe you one for last night — "

The words ended in a grunt. In the middle of the sentence he pivoted fast toward me, bringing up his beefy arm and slamming his right fist at my chin. He almost got it.

I ducked, turning, and his knuckles bounced off my ear. The sound of his fist landing was an explosion inside my head and the impact pushed me a little off balance. Just a little. But he was way off balance, pulled forward by the force of his swing.

By the time he'd started to straighten up I had my feet planted and was swinging at him, a solid left jab that landed on his forehead. Beyond him I could see Hale scrambling to his feet, hand digging under his coat. That left wasn't the hardest punch I ever threw, but it was hard enough to pop Scalzo into the pool.

Fortunately — for me — on his way backward one of Scalzo's flailing arms banged into Hale's battered face, staggering him. Hale's leg hit the chaise longue behind him and he flopped on it, a .45-caliber Army Colt in his hand catching the sunlight.

Scalzo went over the pool's edge, lit in the water with a huge splash. Hale leaned forward, starting to snap the heavy automatic toward me, but by then my own .38 was in my hand. I threw my fist toward him, finger tightening on the trigger.

Neither of us said a word. But he saw me in a crouch, the gun's muzzle trained on his chest. He froze, his automatic still aimed a foot or two away from me. I don't know how long we stayed that way — and, I'll wager, neither did Hale. It couldn't have been long, because Scalzo was still under the pool's surface, and there was a lot of swirling but no more splashing yet.

I said, "Throw it into the pool, Hale."

He licked his lips.

"Throw it."

He let out his breath in a shuddering sigh, and tossed the Colt into the water just as Scalzo's head popped above the pool's surface.

If the sound he was making wasn't the battle honk of a bull moose, it would do till a real moose came along and honked. It was a great, hoarse, crescendoing ululation, accompanied by terrific splashing and kicking as Scalzo clawed the water, clawing in my direction.

It's time to get the hell out of here, I thought.

I turned and started back alongside the house, headed for my Cad. Leaning against the rear wall was the blonde in her pink Bikini. Her eyes were pretty wide.

As I passed she said, "Well, I guess I'd better finish my sunbath. Too bad you can't stick around." And her voice, this time, would not have frozen alcohol in thermometers.

"Yeah," I said. "Isn't it?"

Behind me was a great splashing, and much whooping and yowling. I did not stick around.

:

Thirteen

I left my Cad in a lot at Hollywood Park, as near to the main grand-stand entrance as I could get, a few minutes after 11 A.M. First post wasn't until one-thirty this afternoon, but hundreds of cars were in the lots, early birds already here, working over their forms and charts and dreaming of long-shot parlays.

Colorful pennants atop the grandstand rippled in a light breeze as I paid my admission and went through the turnstile, headed toward the rotunda. At their small stands under striped umbrellas, men were hawking *Racing Forms*, programs, pencils. Saturday, a big day at the track; everything under way even at this hour.

The man I was looking for was Dave Carter, chief of Hollypark's track-security detail — more accurately, the Thoroughbred Racing Protective Bureau, or TRPB, which polices plant and personnel for member tracks of the Thoroughbred Racing Association. Dave, like many others in the TRPB, was an ex-FBI agent. That did not, how-ever, make him a splendid judge of horses. I had not only known him for years, but he had — jokingly, I guess — generously given me three hot tips so far this season, the hottest being a horse named Flyaway, which finished fourth in a ten-horse sprint, the other two sure things coming in last and next-to-last in their races. So I figured he owed me a favor. Besides, he would be interested in what I had to tell him.

I found Dave in his office at the end of the Operations Tunnel. I told him I was checking up on the death of John Kay, gave him a sketchy idea of the background of the case, and repeated what Murphy had so recently told me.

Dave was a tanned, round-faced, medium-size man, affable and easygoing — unless crossed. He listened quietly while I talked, then said without surprise, "A bug, huh?"

"Sure. Little speaker in his ear, wire leading down his coat sleeve to a power pack and receiver in his brief case, maybe even a miniature recorder. And a compact wireless transmitter somewhere here at the track."

"Which covers three hundred and fifty acres. But we might be able to narrow it down for you, Shell." He chewed on his lip for a moment. "You figure whoever killed Kay spotted the ear speaker and knew what it was, or knew *who* John Kay was, and shot him?"

"Or found the transmitter, then tumbled to what Kay was up to. Look, we know he was wearing a hearing aid and carrying a brief case, neither of which items was on him when your men and the local police checked him over. It figures either he dumped the stuff before he was shot, or his killer did later. If so, it might have been turned in to your lost-and-found department." I stopped.

"Go on," Dave said quietly.

"Hell, that's it. I figure Kay was probably sitting where he could not only listen to whatever characters he was bugging but could watch them at the same time and know for sure who was talking. Well, he was sitting with Murphy. So where was Murphy sitting?"

"I'll show you. But take a look at the lost-and-found stuff first. You were right about the bug and brief case." He jerked a thumb at closed locker doors in the wall. "They were turned in here Thursday, after the ninth race."

"Well, damn you. Why didn't you tell me sooner?"

He grinned. "I wanted you to tell *me* a little more first, Shell. One look at the equipment and it was clear *somebody* was using a wireless rig here at the track, but it could have been any of forty thousand people. There wasn't any evidence pointing to a specific person. Not until now."

You wouldn't believe what there is to be found in a lost-and-found department at a race track. You wouldn't believe people could lose all those things. On a good day, though, as many as sixty to seventy thousand people watch the ponies run, and sometimes they get all excited. So excited, in fact, that the items at the moment included wallets, crutches, an inner tube, an artificial leg, a dollar bill, two pairs of

94

women's pink pants, a ticket for a recent "Matsonia" sailing, and among a great variety of other unclaimed goodies, one set of false teeth and three pairs of protuberant falsies.

The important items to me, naturally, were a small ear speaker that looked like a hearing aid, a brief case containing a compact radio receiver complete with two mercury batteries, and finally a sugar-cube-size Tracer Microphone Transmitter, with its twelve-inch antenna extending from one end and from the other a nine-inch battery line tipped with a snap-on battery clip attached to a tiny mercury battery. Traces of some hard, opaque substance were on the base of the transmitter, battery, cable, and antenna — clear evidence that it had been glued or cemented to something.

"That takes care of Kay's deafness," I said. "Have you tried the setup?"

"Sure. It's a good unit, works fine if you keep it away from metal. But don't forget, almost everything here that isn't cement is metal."

"I've a hunch he was bugging a box, Dave. They're steel, aren't they?"

"Right. And if that little mike was close to steel, transmission would be very greatly reduced."

"Uh-huh. Which may be another reason why Kay would have had to be close to his people. Well, let's try it out. Where was Murphy sitting?"

"Come on, I'll show you."

We walked out of the tunnel and then left through the Clubhouse gate, past the bronze statue of Swaps in the Clubhouse entrance gardens, then up the double escalators and into the Clubhouse.

Dave led the way down one of the aisles, stopped, and pointed below us and to our right. "There's Murphy's box," he said, "where Kay was sitting that day."

I looked around. We were standing at the end of Aisle 2, the finish line to our left, slightly left and below us the paddock and winners' circle. It had turned into a beautiful day, clear and cloudless, warm for May. The brown oval of the one-mile track enclosed the vivid green infield, bright banks of flowers accenting the cool smoothness of the infield lakes. On our right were rows of individual chairs comprising the reserved-seat or loge section. Below them and stretching to the right, and also massed to our left, were the painted mustard-yellow boxes, in each of which were four cushioned metal chairs. Farther left and below, on the ground level in front of the grandstand, was where John Kay had been shot.

"O.K.," I said. "Now, do you know if a man named Matthew Wyndham has a box here?"

"Not offhand. I can check it."

"How about Axel Scalzo?"

He raised his eyebrows. "Scalzo? Yeah, he's got a box." Dave pointed to our left. "Down there. Had it for the last five or six seasons. Why are you interested in Scalzo?"

"Kay might have been checking up on him."

"Oh." He shook his head, eyes sober. "Scalzo, huh?" He glanced right, at the Murphy box, then to his left again, measuring the distance. "Pretty close, but I don't know. Everything's metal and cement here, Shell."

"Wait a minute." I'd spotted something. At the front of each box were double shelves five or six feet long with about six inches of open space between them. They provided places where the racegoers could put their programs, charts, drinks. "Those little shelves, Dave. They don't look like metal."

"You're right, they're wood. Only wood anywhere around here."

"Well, if I were doing it, I'd cement my mike and battery inside one of those things, beneath the top shelf."

"Damned close to the steel in front of the box, Shell."

"Yeah, but at least there's no metal above or below where the bug would be. Which is Scalzo's box?"

We went down a couple of steps and left along a narrow cement walk. The third or fourth box from the aisle where we'd been standing had a small name plate affixed to its back: AXEL SCALZO. I stepped inside, kneeled in the front of the box, and ran my fingers along the underside of the top shelf. Nothing. If the little microphone transmitter, antenna, and battery had been affixed there, some trace of the glue or cement should have remained. But I couldn't feel anything.

I looked at the name plates of the boxes on each side of Scalzo's. On the left was George M. Williams, on the right, Arthur Mayberry. I stepped into the Williams box and checked the shelf there. This time it was easy; I found what I was after.

I showed Dave the little hunk of glue or mucilage I'd peeled off the wood. "Some kind of cement," I told him. "The whole transmitter, with antenna and battery cable, would cover a straight line about twenty-two inches long, and I could feel this stuff under the shelf for roughly that distance."

Dave took the transmitter from his pocket and compared the gunk on it with the bit of dried cement. "Looks like the same stuff all right," he said.

"Chemical analysis should prove it, but this is good enough for me," I said. "So who was Kay bugging — Williams or Scalzo? Who's this George M. Williams, anyway?"

"I don't know. I'll look it up for you though."

We went back down to his office and checked his records. The box had been rented for the season, and payment made by mail, by George M. Williams of $1015^1/_2$ Laurel Way, Beverly Hills. Which didn't mean anything to me. Not yet. While we were at it we checked on Axel Scalzo. He had also made payment for his box by mail, had for several years, from his home in the 2300 block of Hollyridge Drive — where I'd so recently been, socking him. It was interesting to me that both Scalzo and Williams had made application for their boxes this season on the same day.

"Let's try out that mike and receiver, O.K.?" I said to Dave, "See if it works?"

He nodded and we went back up to the Clubhouse. With the Tracer Microphone Transmitter, complete with antenna and battery, resting on the bottom shelf in the front of one of the boxes, Dave began speaking in a normal tone. I moved away from him, carrying the receiver in the brief case and with the hearing-aid speaker in my ear. The signal was weak, but carried for several yards before fading out completely. Reception was pretty good under these circumstances.

I gave all the equipment back to Dave, thanked him for his help, and he went back to his office. I smoked a cigarette, thinking, then found a pay phone and called Matthew Wyndham's office at Universal Electronics.

Doody's voice came on.

"Hello, Doody," I said. "Shell Scott."

"Oh, Shellie. What happened to you last night? Was Mr. Scalzo *mad!* I thought he was going to kill somebody or something."

"I'm sure that's what he had in mind. And still does. Doody, is your boss there?"

"Mr. Wyndham?"

"Who else?"

"He didn't come in today. He phoned and said he wouldn't be in."

"I don't suppose he said why."

"No, just he wouldn't be in. Shell, what happened to you last night? You were standing there, then zowie — "

"Well . . . maybe we'll talk about it later. For now, I'm interested in Wyndham."

"Why?"

"I want to ask him some exciting questions, O.K.? Listen, do you happen to know if he ever goes to the race track?"

"Race track?" She was silent for several seconds. "Why do you want to know that?"

"I just have a hunch he does, that's all. And it's important for me to be sure."

"Why?"

"Doody . . . you know I'm a detective, right?"

"Yes, you told me, but — "

"Well, I'm detecting. See? Look, you're his secretary. I assume, if he intends to be at the track, or his club, or on a picnic in Cucamonga, he might so inform you. Right?"

"Sometimes. Where's Cucamonga?"

"It's . . . not important. It was just a figure of . . . Doody, does Wyndham ever come out here to Hollywood Park?"

"Out here, you said. Is that where you're at?"

I sighed. "Yes. Doody, I'm having a frustrating time getting an answer to a simple question. If you don't know — "

"But I do know." She was silent for a few seconds again. "But I don't know if I should tell you."

"You don't, huh? That's nice. Why — "

"You see, he didn't tell me. I just knew he does go to the races sometimes. I happened to see him once."

It started puzzling me a little bit then. "You just happened to?"

"Yes. Last Saturday. I don't know anything about horses, but I'm terribly lucky. And I went to the races last Saturday with a friend, and I just happened to see Mr. Wyndham."

"With a friend. It wouldn't have been Dan — Dr. Noble, would it?"

"Oh, no. I only met Dr. Noble a few days ago. Last night was the first time I went out with him."

"That's good. I guess. Where was Wyndham sitting when you saw him? In one of the boxes?"

"Boxes. Is that like down in front, the reserved places?"

"You've got it."

"That's where he was, then."

"With anybody? Or was he alone?"

"No. I mean, he wasn't with anybody."

"Can you describe where he was sitting?"

"Golly, no. I'd have to show you."

"Well, that won't — "

"I mean, even if I told you where he was, you wouldn't know where he was. I'm terrible with directions. I don't even know where north is, except it's away from south. If you're there I'll come out and show you. If it's important."

"It's important, but — "

"Besides, I want to ask you about last night."

"I'd kind of like to ask you about last night too, but — "

"And I was just leaving anyway. I only work till noon Saturdays, and I can even leave a little early — "

"But — "

"I can be there in a jiffy. You can tell me what happened last night, and we can have fun talking like we did before. That was fun, wasn't it?"

"Well, yes. But — "

"And we can even play the races. Shell, I'm so *glad* you asked me."

"Asked?"

"I was afraid, after last night, you might not want to, maybe you'd be mad at me or something. I'll be there in a jiffy."

"But — "

"Bye, hon." She hung up.

I looked at the phone for a while, and said, "But — " and then slowly clunked the receiver back on its hook.

Well, it wasn't exactly a tragedy. And I wasn't going any place else for a while anyway. Besides, Doody puzzled me more than a little. And I did want to ask her about last night, and what had happened after I'd charged out of the South Seas — among other things. So, I would do what I'd told Gabriel Rothstein I was going to do: play it by ear.

Doody arrived so soon she must have driven at criminal speed from Los Angeles to Inglewood. She arrived all in a flutter, but while fluttering she did point out the box where she'd seen Matthew Wyndham sitting last Saturday.

It figured. And the picture was losing some of its fuzziness. It was, of course, the "Williams" box, right next to Axel Scalzo's.

Fourteen

I paid for reserved seats in the loge section near where Dave and I had been standing earlier, and Doody and I had a sandwich, then returned to our seats as customers began to come in and get settled for the day's races. Scalzo's box was below us to our left, nearer the finish line. It was a bit too close for comfort, but I had to be near enough to see what, if anything, went on down there.

I'd bought copies of the *Daily Racing Form* and programs for both of us, but Doody said she couldn't understand all those figures; she had her own system of picking her horses. "Horsies," she called them, I noticed with a slight shudder. Must be some system, I thought.

When we got settled, there was still half an hour before the first race, so we had time to talk. And right off the bat Doody said, "Isn't it nice I only had to work till noon? It's the union, if you work longer they beat you up or something. I even took off early. The union doesn't mind if you don't work, isn't that funny? Now tell me why you had to know where Mr. Wyndham was sitting last Saturday?"

"Yeah," I said dully, and with that we were off to the races.

I'll say this, physically Doody was a treat, a dream, an eye-balming vision of sparkling brown eyes and rust-blond hair and animated red lips, her astounding body clad superbly in a knit suit — white skirt, white jacket with red slashes on the pockets, white pumps with red toes and heels, red bag in her lap. She looked ready for the races, or the admiral's yacht, or the nineteenth hole at the country club. She was sure great for looking at.

I said, "The reason I want to know where Wyndham sat is because, unless I am out of my mind, which is entirely possible, there's a very good chance he'll be here again today. If so, that will corroborate some

101

of my deductions, and also justify two things I did this morning — namely a remark I made to Axel Scalzo about a doctor, and slamming Axel Scalzo on the conk."

"You sure talk funny," she said.

"I talk — "

"And that doesn't make sense even when you figure it out. What do you mean about a doctor, and slamming a conk, and — "

"Never mind for now, Doody. Maybe we'll talk about it later."

"But I'm really interested, Shell. I really am." Oddly, she sounded very earnest, as if she really was interested.

But I said, "Let's wait and see what happens here in the next hour or so. And you'd better pick your horse in the first race."

"Oh, I've got all mine picked already."

"You've got . . . *all?*"

"Well, nearly. Some I want to ask you about, of course."

"Of course."

Some system, I thought again. But that's what makes horse racing. Around us the seats were filling up, people were marking their programs, looking over the horses being saddled by their trainers in the paddock below us. Bets were already being placed, and every minute and a half the new odds were flashed on the infield Totalisator.

There were several questions I wanted to ask Doody, so without preliminary, I said, "Interesting night last night, Doody. How did you say you met Dr. Noble?"

"He came into the office the first of this week to see Mr. Wyndham. Monday it was. And, well, he saw me — like you did."

"Yeah."

"And we talked for a while. Then Thursday he came in again, and on his way out he asked me for a date. That's all."

"You'd never met him before this week?"

"No. Why?"

"Just curious." I thought a minute. "Doody, I'm going to toss some more names at you. Tell me what you know about each of them, anything you might have heard around the office — or from Dr. Noble, or Axel Scalzo last night, anywhere. O.K.?"

She looked at me calmly, light-brown eyes a little puzzled. Or wary, maybe. "All right."

"Dan Quick."

She shook her head. "I've never heard that name."

"Julie Tangier."

"That I've heard. She's the daughter of the man who went to prison. The one who embezzled the money. Don't you remember, we talked about him last night, Shell?"

"That's right." I paused. "Ardis Ames."

Something changed in her eyes. For the first time. Something, maybe a barely perceptible widening, or a new sharpness deep within her eyes, but a change. She said, though, "I've never heard that name either. Who is she?"

"I wish I knew. When did you meet Scalzo?"

"Last night. Dr. Noble told me we'd go to the South Seas when we made the date, and said he'd introduce me to Mr. Scalzo. Maybe I could get a screen test, and all that."

"Yeah. With Scalzo, 'all that' covers a lot of territory. Well . . . speak of the devil."

I'd spotted Scalzo. He was just entering his box below us and well to our left, flat-faced Hale and me young hood named Deke with him. They got settled in their seats and Scalzo started marking his program.

I wondered if his day at the races had begun the same way last Thursday, the day John Kay had been killed. And if Matthew Wyndham had been sitting near Scalzo then. No sign of Wyndham yet; but I had a hunch he'd show. Well, there was nothing much to do now but wait and see. And in the meantime, Doody and I could place a few bets.

It looked like a good card — and I have a ball at the races ordinarily. While awaiting developments, I might as well enjoy myself, I figured. Maybe I could win back that hundred and twenty-five bucks I'd lost so far on my Universal Electronics stock.

I studied my *Racing Form* for a while, then turned to Doody. "Honey," I said, "if you want a hot tip on the first race, the solid horse is Red Acorn. . . ."

Fifteen

Nuts to Red Acorn.

And precisely the same sentiments to Vapor Trail, King Tuttle, Gay Lovely, Dancearound, and Sirocco. I had lost three hundred and ninety dollars on those nags. Added to the one-hundred-and-twenty-five-dollar UE loss, I was exactly five hundred and fifteen dollars in the hole. In only twenty-four hours at that. I was killing myself — and losing nearly twenty-one-fifty an hour.

The hell with the races. The hell with Wall Street. The hell with capitalism. Down with —

"Oh, this is *fun*," Doody said.

"*Arrggh.*"

"Which horsie do you like in the seventh, Shellie?"

"Let's do it different this time," I said sweetly. "Tell me which horsie *you* like."

"I'm going to bet on Silver Arrow."

"Not . . . Thunder Boy?"

"No. Is he your pick?"

"Well, he was."

This wouldn't do. I was losing my *confidence*. Once you lose your confidence, you're dead. No, by golly, I'd stick to my guns, plunge ahead, go down with banners flying. I'd bet on Thunder Boy — even if Doody *was* three hundred and eighty bucks ahead. It was dumb luck, that's all; I'd stick to *science*. I'd charge up to the sellers window and plunk it all down on Thunder Boy. Yeah! I thought of Marshal Foch at the Battle of the Marne: "My right is driven in. My left has vanished. My center is hard pressed. The situation is excellent. I will attack at once!"

Man, that was it! Attack! I couldn't lose! I was so damn near broke now, the situation was excellent. I was as nuts as Marshal Foch. It thrilled me. Yeah! I would throw sanity to the winds and bet a bundle!

Doody's voice broke in on my thrilling thoughts. "Shell, what's the matter?"

"Matter? Nothing's the matter!"

"You just cried out, 'Attack!' It sounded so strange."

"I'll bet it did." I paused. "Too much, really. After all, it's only a horse race, isn't it?"

"And you were gnashing your teeth, like."

"Like what?"

"Like — in pain. Are you hurting?"

"Boy, am I hurting. I mean, I was thinking."

"It hurts you to think?"

"Don't be ridiculous." I shifted my position haughtily and scraped the still-very-sore spot where I'd been pinked. "Ow," I said, and added, "It only hurts when I sit on my right, uh, side."

"Why?"

"Because I got shot there last night, that's why."

"*Shot?* With a bullet?"

"No, a crossbow. A cannon. A machine gun. Hell, yes, a bullet."

"I didn't know — how did it happen?"

"Two pals of Scalzo's were beating up a friend of mine, and when I appeared they expressed their pique and displeasure by shooting me."

"*There?*"

"There."

"How . . . were you going away from them?"

"No, I was *not* going away from them. I was going *at* them — like Peter Pan, I recall my friend saying. I know this sounds silly, but . . . well . . ."

"How did you get shot there?"

"Don't ask me. I didn't do it. But I was, well, flying through the air in what appears on reflection to have been an awkward position. Anyway, it happened. Doody, do you *really* like Silver Arrow?"

"You say they were friends of Mr. Scalzo's?"

"They sure weren't friends of mine."

"Shell . . ." Her voice was different. "I think I've made a serious mistake."

"Not in the first six races you haven't. What do you mean — are you betting on Thunder Boy? — Hey, now."

I stopped, because that was when I saw Matthew Wyndham. He went straight to the box next to Scalzo's, the "George M. Williams" box. He and Scalzo didn't even look at each other. Not then. Wyndham opened his *Racing Form* and seemed to be studying it.

So it was going to happen. That tied it. Doody hadn't been lying. And there sat Scalzo and Wyndham, cheek by jowl. And soon we would all be eyeball-to-eyeball, and no telling what then. The big pieces fitted together now; not all the little pieces, but maybe I could find them and squeeze them in later. I could feel my pulse beat picking up, the growing pressure in my arteries.

I hadn't decided whether to stroll down and confront that gang or to wait until after the races and tackle them one at a time. Wyndham, I knew, was the softest; he was the cookie about to crumble. If I could find the right spot to apply pressure, and I thought I could.

I was still considering which course to follow when Doody went back to what she'd been saying before. "Shell, please tell me exactly why you're so interested in Mr. Wyndham. You've never really told me, you've avoided it whenever I asked. And I've got to know."

I turned and looked at her. "I didn't tell you because there was a chance you'd pass on everything I said to your boss, and that would have complicated things for me. But it doesn't make any difference now. Your boss is down there with Scalzo at this moment, and I'm soon going to tell him the whole bit myself."

She looked toward Scalzo's box, nibbled her lip. "I hadn't seen him. When did he arrive?"

"Just now. O.K., you want to know, here it is. I think Matthew Wyndham — not Ryder Tangier — swiped the loot from Universal Electronics. I don't know the mechanics, but that's not important. More important is the fact that Scalzo down there does know Matthew Wyndham, does now meet and undoubtedly has before met him — right here, in the paradoxical privacy of a teeming race track. Since Scalzo does *not* want me to reach Wyndham's ear and put a bug in it — about a Dr. Quick, among other things — he had to set up another meet today and most likely at the moment is telling Wyndham to help get me killed, or blow town until the heat's off. The heat I've helped build under those boys, and that John Kay, who got killed for it, started. The fact that Wyndham is chummy with Scalzo is excruciatingly significant because Wyndham is president of UE, and Scalzo is a crook from the word go. His last and only recent arrest was for fixing a horse race, I think he's graduated and is now trying to fix an electronics company, namely UE. And I also think now I'll be able to prove it."

"Shell," she said, "I'm Julie Tangier."

Sixteen

It rocked me.

It hit me so hard and so suddenly that it almost literally made me numb. But it shouldn't have.

Once the words were out of her mouth a dozen things I'd seen or heard, widely separated before, came together into a pattern. And I said slowly, "I should have guessed."

She put her hand on my knee again, leaned close to me. "I didn't tell you before, Shell, because I didn't know who you were, what you were after. We only met yesterday afternoon, remember."

"I sure remember."

"I think Dr. Noble, and perhaps Mr. Wyndham, too, may have begun to suspect who I really am. And just two nights before you and I met, I talked to Mr. Kay, told him who I was and all I'd learned — then the very next day he was killed. I don't know what he might have said before then. He might have revealed who I was, or at least part of what I'd told him. Then one day after his death *you* showed up and said you were a detective too. You could have been lying, working for them, trying to find out how much I knew."

"For them? For those — those gangsters?"

She smiled. "Well, you look like you could be a gangster."

"I do, huh? Fine. Great."

"A nice gangster. I mean you don't look retiring or weak. You look more as if you'd just killed something with a stone ax. After all, Shell, it didn't matter much what you looked like. There are nice-looking criminals too. I had to find out if I could trust you — especially after what happened to Mr. Kay."

I looked at her, and she looked different. She was different. "Hello, Julie," I said. "Hello, Julie Tangier."

She smiled. "Hello, Shell Scott. Incidentally, Doody was really my nickname, when I was about six years old. But I invented Nell Duden."

"I'll stick with Doody then. I kind of got used to Doody, the dumb blonde." I shook my head. "I'm still trying to absorb this. Tell me, do you really speak seven languages, and ride jumping horses and swim and golf and such, and read Plutarch in the original Greek, and split atoms — "

She laughed softly. "I speak the seven languages, Shell, but I don't split atoms — "

"The hell you don't. You sure split some of mine."

I looked at her, still feeling a bit numb. As striking as the rest of it was the change in her voice now, her manner of speaking. It had gone in the bat of an eye from battiness and a somewhat nasal twanginess to a soft, cultured, whispering zippiness. "Wow," I said. "Look, Doody, you'd better fill me in, tell me what you told Kay, the whole story. I've probably got an item or two you'd like to know, too. Together, we might have something."

"All right."

Down on the track the bugler tooted his long trumpet and the horses came onto the track for the seventh race. As Doody talked, they lined up and started walking single file toward the starting gate, a hundred yards or so to our left.

"I was in Paris," Doody said, "when the scandal broke about Dad's embezzlement — alleged embezzlement. I didn't learn of it then. Dad didn't tell me — he wouldn't. You'd have to know him to understand, but he wouldn't have wanted me to worry. By the time I found out what was going on, the trial was almost over. I got back to the States last month, just before he was sentenced. I talked to him twice." She bit her lip. "It was horrible for him, but he didn't complain, just told me he was innocent."

"It looks as if he is."

Her eyes flashed. "Of course he is. But nobody else thought so, not the police, or the jury — nobody. It looked impossible, but I *knew* he was innocent, and if there was any way to prove it, I meant to prove it."

"Like Foch at the Marne," I said, apropos of practically nothing.

She looked at me, one arched brow rising. "After all," she said, "he did win the battle."

"Did he? Well, I'll be damned."

"He did," she said. "And I'll win this one." She smiled. "*I* mean, we will."

I grinned at her. "Sure we will. Go on."

"Miss Brandt — Alice — was very close to Dad and felt sure he was innocent. Even though she couldn't believe Mr. Wyndham guilty, either. Mr. Wyndham and I had never met, and I was able to talk Alice into quitting, so I'd have a chance to get her job. I gave her money for a trip back east. She really is back east, visiting her family."

"Cross off Miss Brandt."

"I thought the most difficult part would be convincing Mr. Wyndham that he should hire me — especially since I'd decided to become, well, Nell Duden. And Nell wasn't the brainiest secretary in the world."

"No kidding."

"But it turned out to be easy. Five-minute interview, and I was hired. I really can't understand it. Of course, Alice did tell me a few things about Mr. Wyndham, that he liked blondes and so forth — which is why I had my red hair lightened." Doody's eyes were merry, I thought. "And probably I should have dressed much more conservatively for the interview."

"The poor old man," I said, rolling my eyes. "He didn't have a chance. Dr. Noble didn't have a chance. I didn't have a chance. You're almost frightening — "

"Anyway," she went on, "as soon as I got the job I just left my hotel and moved into the Lanai Apartments. Some of my gowns and make-up were from Paris, some from Fifth Avenue. Well, I didn't take a thing, not anything that belonged to Julie Tangier. And I became little Nell."

"Yeah. I should have noted that the date of Julie's exit from the Watson-Parker coincided almost precisely with Doody's employment at Universal Electronics."

"Oh. I didn't think about that. I really didn't."

"That helps. Well, what did you find out about Wyndham? I assume that if you had enough to really stick him you'd have gone to the police."

"Yes, but I haven't learned that much yet. I do know, though, that Dr. Noble has some kind of hold over him. I don't know what it is, but it has something to do with the Ardis Ames you mentioned."

"What about her?"

"All I know is, she's dead."

I blinked. "Dead, huh?" Remembering Wyndham's knee-buckling reaction when I'd mentioned her name, I said, "That would fit. How did you find this out?"

"The day after I started working for Mr. Wyndham I stayed late, after he'd left, and rewired the intercom so that his set was always open. Then whenever I opened my key I could hear what was said in his office."

"*You* rewired it?"

"Yes, it was very simple. I just disabled his on-off switch. Don't forget, Shell, I grew up with Dad — with Ryder Tangier, I mean. Instead of teaching me 'There is a cat, it is a Tom cat,' he — "

"Don't tell me. Don't destroy my illusions about dumb womanhood. 'There is a cat,' indeed."

"I was exaggerating."

"I hope so. Dear, I fear we aren't going to get along . . ."

"Yes, we are," she interrupted me gently. "Yes, we are, Shell." And the way she said it, I believed her.

"Go on, what's with this Ardis Ames?" I asked. "And how do you know she's dead?"

"The first time Dr. Noble came into the office — I told you that was last Monday — I heard him say to Mr. Wyndham, 'Just stay in line, Matt. Don't forget, I'm not the only one who knows about Ardis, and knows she's buried in that little plot at Fairlawn.' Something like that. And he didn't say Ardis Ames, just Ardis, but I assume it must be the same girl."

"A reasonable assumption. Incidentally, did you know Dr. Noble isn't a doctor?"

"No." Her light-brown eyes widened.

"Score one for me. He is a confidence man named Daniel Quick, known among the losers as Dandy Dan."

"Well . . . that *is* interesting," she said. "No wonder he made me feel so crawly."

"Oh? You didn't seem to think he was so repulsive last night. When you were ripping off your clothes, or hauling him into your apartment — oh, oh."

"You *followed* us. Why, Shell, you're — "

"I followed *him*. He is a criminal, and it was my duty — "

"You're jealous!"

"What rot." It didn't come off exactly the way I'd thought it would. I tried it again. "What *rot! What* rot. The hell with it."

"If you're interested, he left in half an hour."

"I know."

"What you don't know is that he was furious when he left. You see, when he made the date he specifically mentioned taking me to the South Seas, and explained about the amateur strip contests. He said he had a lot of pull with the club owner, Mr. Scalzo, and could almost guarantee I'd get a screen test."

"'Baby, you should oughta be in pix, kid.'"

"That was the approach. Anyway, it told me what he expected, and I thought if I went along with it — up to a point, of course — he'd be more likely to talk freely with me. So *that's* why I went to the South Seas with him. But afterward, the reason he left my apartment in such a temper, was because I asked too many questions, he said, and gave him all the wrong answers."

"Good for you. *Good* for you."

"He said I got him all . . . well, fermented, with my dance at the South Seas, and then led him on, and then turned him off. He talks like that."

"I'll bet."

"After all, that was the idea. And it worked — until he got furious. But *before* then he did tell me one thing. I said I was worried that Mr. Wyndham might fire me if he found out I was going with him, and dancing and all. And he said he had so much on Mr. Wyndham that Matt would do anything he said, even if I danced in front of the office. Matt would pay me for a year, even if I didn't do any work — if he told him to. I tried to find out what it was he had on Mr. Wyndham, but a little while after that was when he got so furious. He wanted me to . . . . dance again, and I wouldn't."

"Uh-huh. Well, he got so furious he went home to his wife."

"Is he married?"

"I think so. If he isn't, he's giving a good imitation."

The horses were in the starting gate now. All except one that was giving the boy a little trouble. But they'd be off and running in a minute or so. It was five o'clock on the nose.

Doody said, "I'd hoped to learn more from him, Shell. After hearing him talk to Mr. Wyndham that way — in a really overbearing, threatening manner — I felt it was at least possible Dr. Noble was blackmailing him. And if he *had* been, perhaps Mr. Wyndham had taken money from the firm in order to pay him off. Almost every cent Mr. Wyndham has is in joint accounts with his wife, which means she would know if he made any large withdrawals. And she's extremely frugal, watches what he spends like a hawk — so he told me one afternoon when he was convincing me his wife didn't understand him."

"All that I can believe. I've met the lady. I'd say you did extremely well with your little intercom, Doody. And, uh, other factors. Anything else?"

"Just one thing. Last Saturday a man — I don't know who he was — phoned Mr. Wyndham. I was listening in my office. He said he had a tip on the fifth race at Hollywood Park, and hung up. It seemed odd because that was all he said. It made me wonder if Mr. Wyndham was betting on the races, so when he left the office I followed him, or tried to. I lost him in Inglewood, but it seemed certain he was coming to the race track here."

"So you came out alone, huh? Not with a date."

She nodded. "I just came in and started looking for him. I didn't find him for almost an hour. He was sitting where I showed you — but nobody was in the other box then. I mean, Mr. Scalzo and those men weren't there then."

"Probably showed up for the fifth race. Wednesday night you told Kay all this? Including where Wyndham was sitting?"

"Yes. I'd noticed the name plate on his box. I didn't tell you that, Shell, because I wanted to come out, wanted to know what you were doing here."

"Uh-huh. Doody, you said something about not being sure your cover — the Nell Duden identity — is holding up. What about that?"

"When Dr. Noble — Dan Quick, I mean — came out of Mr. Wyndham's office last Monday I was listening on my intercom. Mr. Wyndham was on the phone, and I hadn't expected anyone to come out right then. Well, Dr. Noble could surely hear Mr. Wyndham's voice coming over my speaker. I hit my key as soon as I could, and tried to divert his attention — the way I did with you — but I'm not sure whether it worked or not."

"If it didn't he's made of sterner stuff than I am. I remember hearing Wyndham's phone ring myself when I walked into your office yesterday, Doody. But right after that something distracted me and I plain failed to consider the significance of that bell and voice." I grinned at her. "Something about a girdle you weren't wearing, wasn't it?"

She smiled. "Something like that. There's this too. I asked so many questions of Dr. Noble last night that once he calmed down and thought about it, there's a possibility he started wondering why. If he has sense enough to put two and two together . . ."

"He probably does. He's not a dumb hood, Doody. He is a very sharp con man, not a bit stupid."

"Well, in that case . . ." She hesitated only a moment, then her expression changed ever so slightly, got a bit blank, and her voice went up to a higher, thinner pitch. "In that case, Shellie," she said, "if you want to come to the aid of a lady in distress, I'm in it."

It killed me. It was dumb Doody in the flutter of a long eyelash, the bat of a sizzling eye. Another of those sappy Doodyisms — only not sappy. Not at all.

Looking back at the times we'd been together, I remembered her habit of occasionally hesitating, pausing briefly before speaking. I'd felt those were the moments when her poor little mind went blank and she had to wait for the electricity to come on again. But now I realized what those pauses had meant. In those blank spaces she hadn't been unconscious. She'd been *thinking!*

"You're a freak," I said.

"Well," she said — pause — "people are so inhuman, aren't they?"

I looked at her, shaking my head. "Doody," I said, "you're marvelous, and I love you to pieces — both of you — but you are lousing me up. You are destroying my Doody."

She batted her eyelashes. "Better to have loved and loused," she said sweetly, "then never to have loved at all."

"*Quit* it, will you?" I paused, thinking. I would have had a clever reply to her last comment — in about a hundred years — only right then the track announcer cried: "The flag is up!" Then, almost immediately: "Theeere they go!"

The first subdued roar went up from the crowd.

"At the start, it's Thunder Boy going to the front. . . ."

I jerked my head around and, oddly, instead of the sprinting horses I saw a face. It was a face that lit the fuses on all my glands. Striding along the cement walk behind the boxes, then leaning in to speak to Axel Scalzo, was the guy with black brows and eyes and scarred lip, the sonofabitch who'd shot me last night, then clanged me on the head. The guy who was not, if I could help it, going to get away from me again.

Seventeen

I stood up.

"What's the matter?" Doody asked me.

"There's the mug who shot me last night. The mug who is soon going to be damned sorry he shot me."

Doody put her hand on my arm. "Shell, wait."

"Wait, hell." I was wound up like a six-foot alarm clock, blood thumping in me, and I could feel the beat building, warming my face. I shrugged Doody's hand off my arm and started toward the man.

And right then he turned and saw me. Or, rather, saw me again, for undoubtedly he'd seen me earlier. Because he was looking up at me as he turned, pointing, and the whole gang was looking where he pointed. That was probably why the creep had gone down there, to tip Scalzo that he'd spotted me.

The noise of the crowd was louder now.

"Around the first turn, it's Thunder Boy by one length, Stimulator second by a nose, and Silver Arrow . . ."

I climbed over people's feet, jumped down to the walk behind the back row of boxes. I saw Scalzo yank the man close, saying something, then the creep turned and sprinted along the walk, away from me.

I was gaining on him as I went past Scalzo's box, and all my attention — too much of my attention, it turned out — was on the running man. Because suddenly I stopped gaining on him. Somebody stuck out a foot and I ran into it. My legs didn't exactly go out from under me, but they didn't go anywhere near where I meant them to, and then the hard cement came up at me. I saw it hit my outstretched hands and keep on coming toward my face.

I landed heavily, skidded for six feet, arching my neck and holding my pained expression up off the cement. It saved my face, but angled my head enough so it clanged into one of the round metal posts of the rail behind the boxes. The sound of my head clanging on steel seemed to echo inside my skull, getting fainter and slower like an alarm-clock bell running down. The crowd noise grew softer, then slowly started increasing in volume again.

I got to my feet, swung around. Hale stood where he'd been when he'd hooked my ankle with his foot and tripped me, leg still stuck out in front of him. Close on my right was Deke. He held his coat in his hands, right hand out of sight. He jabbed the coat forward and I could feel what had to be a gun dig into my back. He shoved me close to Scalzo's box. I was still dazed from the smack on my skull, not completely coordinated. Only a few seconds had passed from the moment I'd fallen until now, as I stood, head ringing, looking at Scalzo's sour face.

Then it was as if a valve opened in my head. The crowd noise slammed against my eardrums as my hearing came all the way back to normal. Everything got a little sharper. The track announcer's voice boomed over the yelling around me:

"Passing the half-mile post it's Thunder Boy and Stimulator, Thunder Boy by a neck, Stimulator second by half a length, Go-No-Go by two lengths, and Silver Arrow . . ."

On the edge of my vision I could see the blur of bright racing silks spread out on the far side of the track like something in an abstract painting.

Scalzo merely glanced at me. "Get him away from here," he said, looking past me to Deke. Then he flicked his eyes to Hale, nodded silently. I knew what that meant — or, rather, what it was supposed to mean. But it didn't; not this time, it didn't.

Deke's gun dug into my back, harder, sliding over my spine. I braced my legs, stood there.

Scalzo moved his head, shiny scalp gleaming dully, large pale eyes staring into mine. He wore a gray coat and open sports shirt beneath it, tufts of wiry hair showing at the hollow of his throat.

"It's no good, Scalzo," I said. "If you do it at all, you do it right here. Where it'll tag you."

On my left, in the adjacent box, Matthew Wyndham stood, his expression one of near panic. His open mouth was pulled down at its corners, eyes wide, wrinkles in his forehead and at the bridge of his nose.

I looked at Scalzo again. "It won't work twice, you bastard. It wouldn't have worked with Kay if he'd thought you were going to kill him. And it sure as hell won't work with me."

Wyndham let out a sigh and sank into his seat as if his legs had become too weak to support his weight.

I glanced around. Incredibly, it seemed to me, nobody was looking at us. All eyes were on the track and most of the people were on their feet. From their point of view all that had happened was that a man had fallen, was now standing talking to another man. There hadn't been any real violence — not yet. And the horses were coming around the turn, heading for the stretch.

Scalzo was silent briefly, then leaned toward me. "It don't make no difference. You're dead." I could see his mouth moving, forming the words, but could barely hear him over the yelling of the crowd. "So it happens right here, so what?" he went on, lips thinning. "The boys will get lost and I'll be clean enough. A beef, sure. Nothing I can't handle." His eyes widened slightly and he looked at Wyndham. "Matt, get out of here. Beat it!"

Wyndham got slowly to his feet, turned, and walked away from us, moving like a man in a trance.

I hadn't really been worried until that moment. It seemed almost insane to think Scalzo would have his men shoot me here, in the middle of these thousands of people, especially right next to his own box. But maybe . . .

"Turning into the stretch . . ."

They were in the stretch now, in the run for the wire. And a man isn't really aware of how loud the sound is from thousands of throats, during that run for the money, unless he's giving his attention to that sound itself instead of to the movement and action on the track. It hammered the ears, like a continuing explosion. A shot, muffled, wouldn't be heard. Maybe not even by me.

Earlier I'd been warm, beat of blood in artery and flow in vein flushing my skin, heating my face. But now in the space of a heartbeat I felt the chill spreading over me — a chill I'd felt before. It was like a cold breath on my skin, and with it came the familiar intensifying of sight and sound, sharpening of sense and perception.

The crowd sound around me became not merely a jumbled roar but thousands of individual voices blending. Scalzo's eyes were wide and staring and I could see tiny red veins in the gray iris, note wrinkles in his pursed lips and cracks at the edges of his mouth.

On my left Wyndham was still moving, just starting up the steps. I could hear the drumming of hoofs. I could see the red and green and yellow and orange, blue and pink of the jockeys' silks, see the number 7 on the horse in the lead. And with a separate part of my mind I knew that seven was Thunder Boy, half a length in front. Over the P.A. speaker came: "Moving up fast on me outside is Silver Arrow . . ."

But most of my mind was filled with what I was going to do, in fact with what I was doing, because suddenly I was doing it.

In a normal situation Deke would never have shoved his gun into my back and left it there, not where I could feel it, know where the gun was and where he was. But this wasn't a normal situation. Hale was moving toward me when I turned sharply to my right and plunged my right arm backward in the same movement. My elbow hit Deke's fist under my wadded coat, jarred it and the gun away from me. I kept turning, raising my right arm, swinging my left foot around and planting it as I faced Deke. He was inches away, arm angled across his body. I threw my open hand down with all my strength and its edge hammered his wrist. The gun was falling as I slapped my left foot back and turned, swinging that right hand up again before I even saw Hale.

When I saw his face he was almost on me, arms out stretched, but my right hand was in a fist by then and the fist was moving. It moved up between his hands and landed under the point of his chin. He spun like a man hit by a bullet.

Something grabbed me, tripped me. I fell onto my side. A fist slammed my head, banged it hard against the concrete. I squirmed around as Deke hit me again, got a hand on my throat, thumb digging violently, painfully against my windpipe. My vision blurred momentarily, but I could see his other hand move, fingers curling around the butt of his gun lying on the cement.

Probably neither of us thought of the crowd, the people who now were almost surely watching. I know I didn't. I was still on my side, pain roaring in my head, right arm against my chest. I forced the arm up, squeezed my fingers around the butt of my .38.

Deke's thumb felt as if it were poking a hole in my throat. He swung the big automatic toward my face. It loomed ridiculously large in front of my eyes, inches from my forehead. The gun was aimed at my skull and his finger was on the trigger. But my own Colt was in my hand and I was trying to shove my hand clear into his gut.

I pulled the trigger twice.

The sound was very faint, like sticks breaking. His face hung in the air near me, features twisted, lips pressed together. Then slowly, like a man starting to smile, his expression softened. The lips relaxed, became more full, the corners of his mouth moved up a little. He still held the gun near my head, but slowly his features smoothed, and then the gun drooped, came to rest on my chest.

I shoved him away from me, onto his back. He moved like rags. As I got to my feet he lay still, but his eyes rolled, slanted toward me. His chin hung slack, and a little blood oozed up from inside him, spilled over the corner of his mouth and down the side of his jaw. Then his eyes moved for the last time, with a little jerk, and were still.

It had all happened so swiftly that the track announcer was just calling the names of Thunder Boy and Silver Arrow, and after them the third and fourth horses. Scalzo looked down at Deke's body, then his eyes raised to my face.

The gun was still in my fist. I stepped toward him, leaned over the rail and grabbed the front of his coat in my other hand.

"Don't pull that trigger," he said rapidly. "It'd be murder. Don't do it, Scott."

The sound died suddenly around us. The race was over, fans returning to normal. Near us a woman screamed. I looked up and saw a tiny middle-aged woman across the aisle and above us, looking down over the rail at Deke's body. Her mouth was still open, but she screamed only that once. She stared at the stain of blood on Deke's shirt. A man swore aloud. Other voices were raised then, in question or shocked comment, a spreading circle of voices around us.

"The placing judges have called for a photo," the announcer was saying. "Please hold all tickets until the results of the race are declared official."

I put my gun away.

Sweat was beaded on Scalzo's forehead. He said thickly, "It would've been murder, Scott. Just like this was." He nodded toward Deke. "I'll swear that's what this was."

"It wouldn't stick and you know it."

Behind me a man said loudly, "He shot him. I saw the gun. He shot him."

I swung my head around and spotted him, a red-faced man with abundant brown hair, stiff finger pointing. He shut up suddenly. But a lot of eyes were on me now.

Scalzo said, "Sure. And you're real thick with the local fuzz. But they'd hold you, Scott. And it might stick. You know I've got pull, you punk sonofabitch. But even you don't have any idea how much pull."

He looked past me, up and to his left, and smiled. I didn't know what he had to smile about. But I was beginning to think I didn't have much to smile about either. I *had* killed a man, and it was a sure thing that more than a handful of people had seen me do it. Witnesses are funny. They'd remember my shooting the man, all right, and especially my standing up, standing over him with a gun in my hand. And maybe they'd remember what had happened before that, remember what the other man had done, the gun aimed at my head.

Maybe. But for all I knew, fifteen people here might swear I'd stabbed Deke in hot blood. Not that any of the charges would actually stick, but they could get sticky. Especially since it is a psychological truism that once people have made an accusation, they immediately start convincing themselves that the charge is absolutely true.

Hale moved one of his feet. Then he groaned softly. Scalzo glanced up and beyond me again as he had before, and smiled again. Then he said to me, "You lose, killer. I got you where I want you, you punk sonofabitch."

Well, I'd warned him. I'd even let his last foul-mouthed crack at me pass without comment. I might do that once; but this made twice.

While he was still smirking, I hauled off and slammed a fist into his smirk. It was a good blow; I got my weight solidly behind it and his lips peeled open. He bounced backward, hit the front of his box and slumped. I didn't wait to see if he got up.

I headed back up the steps. I was in a hurry, but I didn't run. There'd been quite enough action just now to suit me, but it hadn't really taken much time, not clock time anyway.

The race had been over for less than a minute; and the time of the race itself had been one minute and forty-two seconds. It was only about a minute since I'd shot Deke; it might be another minute before the real hue and cry began. And it had been at most three minutes since I'd spotted the guy with the scarred lip. . . .

Yeah, that creep. What had happened to him?

I remembered Scalzo saying something to him as I'd headed that way, then the guy had taken off like a rabbit. Taken off, but for where? Well, that would keep; I'd find him.

I started toward the seat where I'd left Doody.

Only Doody was gone.

Eighteen

It was well past 6 P.M., and I was parked on a side street off Manchester, two or three blocks from Western Avenue and a few miles from Hollywood Park. My gun was reloaded, six slugs in the chambers; I was ready to go — but with no place to go. And I was alone. I hadn't found Doody.

After discovering she was gone, I'd run down the Clubhouse stairs to the ground floor and cut through the Winner's Circle food bar, then down the curving ramp and outside. There'd still been a good deal of confusion back there around Deke's body, I guess; at least nobody had stopped me. I'd tried to check cars leaving, but there were thousands of cars and it was an impossible job. I'd even gotten a hat and dark glasses from the trunk of my Cadillac and gone back into the Clubhouse to check our seats again from a distance. But there'd been no sign of Doody — or of Scalzo, either, by then.

Doody wouldn't have been cashing tickets on the seventh race; I hadn't bought any tickets on the seventh. And if she'd left for a minute or two she would have come back to our seats right away. No, either she'd simply left, taken off of her own free will, or — the only alternative — she'd left unwillingly.

That scar-lipped hood, of course, had spotted me with Doody. And Scalzo had been telling him something before he'd run. Besides that, I remembered Scalzo's glances up into the stands — toward the reserved-seat section where Doody and I had been sitting — and his self-satisfied smiles.

If Scalzo's man — and maybe Scalzo himself by now — had Doody, did they still think she was fluttery, harmless Nell Duden? Or did they suspect, perhaps even know, that she was Julie Tangier?

My palms kept sweating and muscles in my stomach were hard with tension. I had already phoned the Lanai Apartments in Hollywood: Miss Duden had left early in the morning and had not yet returned. I called Scalzo's home on Hollyridge Drive but the phone rang unanswered. I even called the Watson-Parker and talked to my contact there; no soap, nothing. Maybe it was too soon. I still didn't accept the possibility that Scalzo had Doody, but I couldn't get it out of my mind. And I had to ask myself what it meant if he did.

If he knew she was Julie Tangier, there was a damned good chance he'd just kill her. But my being alive, knowing he might have her, would complicate that part of it for him. So if he did have her, it seemed likely he'd keep her alive at least until I was out of the way, no longer a threat to him. If I knew Scalzo, anyway; and I thought I knew him well enough.

And if I did know him, if I was right, there was a way to find out for sure. Scalzo would be anxious for me to know he had her. He'd be almost as anxious to reach me as I was to get my hands on him.

So I made another call, this time to the Spartan Apartment Hotel.

Jimmy, the night man, was on the desk. "Shell, Jimmy. Any calls for me?"

"Yeah. Some guy, he's called every ten minutes for the last half hour. Last time was just a couple minutes ago."

"He leave any number for me to call back?"

"That's the funny thing. Every time he calls he gives me a different number."

"It's not funny, Jimmy. Probably they're different pay phones."

"You know what it's all about, huh?"

"I think so. What was the last number?"

He gave it to me and I hung up, dialed the number.

I knew the voice as soon as he said hello. "This is Hale, Scott. You make a squeal to the fuzz yet?"

That answered all of my questions. Or at least all of them but one. "No," I said.

"Don't."

"Go on."

"There's a couple things Axel wants you to do instead, and you better do them, Scott. Just like he says."

"Or?"

"Or we kill the girl."

I felt my mouth getting dry; my blood seemed to cool a little, sending a slow chill over my skin. And the next thing Hale said answered that last question.

"Yeah, we've got the girl," he said. "We've got Julie."

Nineteen

I didn't say anything.

Hale waited, then went on, "In case you think this ain't on the level, here's how it was. Soon as Luke spotted you with the babe he tells the boss, and right away Axel tells Luke to grab the twist and hustle her out, we'd hang onto you long enough so he could pull it off. She's with Axel right now. No sense you lookin', he's takin' her to his safe pad. So play ball or she gets killed that much quicker."

In Hale's language, the "safe pad" would simply be another house — or maybe apartment, cabin, anything — where Scalzo could be safe, could lie low when his usual hangouts got too hot for him. It's a not-uncommon precaution among hoodlums, and Scalzo was a hoodlum. But Hale had told me something else, maybe, without meaning to. He'd said Scalzo was "taking" Julie there, not that they were there now. Which probably meant they were on their way, or had been when Hale started phoning the Spartan. Which almost surely meant it wasn't in Inglewood.

"No sense you lookin', Scott," Hale went on. "Only three of us besides the boss knows where the pad is."

"So what am I supposed to do? Go stand on a corner where you bastards can shoot me?"

"Oh, nothing like that, Scott," he said with oily sincerity.

"The boss knows you wouldn't go for nothing like that. Just two easy things. First, you keep your mouth zippered. Second, there's a plane leaving tonight from L.A. International, for Mexico City. You take the plane, that's all. A ticket's waiting there for you. By the time you get back — if you're dumb enough to come back — everything'll be under control here."

126

Sure. It was only a little better than a street corner. It could have been Burbank Airport instead of L.A. International, or a depot, bus station — any place where they knew I'd be. They had to know where I was going to be, and approximately when I'd be there, before they could be reasonably sure of killing me.

"Generous of Scalzo," I said.

"Hell, you got him over a barrel, kind of. And Scott, crack wise if you want to, but do it. Don't think killing the babe bothers him."

"I don't."

"You try to tip the fuzz, or toss your weight around, she's dead. Wouldn't be no strain either. Nobody knows we got her — nobody but you. And anything you'd say wouldn't make no difference, you couldn't prove nothing, Scott. Nice and clean, she just turns up dead."

She'd turn up dead anyway, now that they knew who she was. Even if they let me catch that plane, which they wouldn't, she'd be dead before it got a hundred feet in the air.

"When does the plane take off?" I asked him.

"Seven-fifteen."

It was a little after six-thirty now. "Hell, that's less than forty-five minutes," I said. "That's not enough time — "

"It's all the time you got, Scott. You can make it — so long as you go straight there, and don't try nothing funny."

"How do I know she's alive?"

"You don't, I guess. But she is. Axel said if you got to be convinced, he'd let her phone you, so's you'll know she's O.K."

"At the airport?"

"That's right. Just before you climb aboard."

I swallowed. "I told you, that's too soon. I can't — "

"Knock it off, Scott. You got no choice." He paused, then went on deliberately. "Axel said to make a big point of this. The Tangier girl is alive — even if she knows too goddamn much already. But if you don't answer that call when you're paged at the airport, she *won't* be alive no more. The boss'll know you're trying to cross him, and right then, Scott, *right then*, we take the girl out in the hills." He chuckled. "Such a good-lookin' sweet-stacked twist, though, maybe first we have ourselves a little fun with her."

"You sonofa — " I cut it off. Hale didn't say anything.

127

I licked my lips, but my lips stayed dry. Finally I said, "All right, Hale. Have her call me at exactly seven-ten, five minutes before take-off. And Hale, if she doesn't call, I won't be on that plane. I'll be looking for you and Scalzo. You tell Scalzo that."

"Yeah."

"So be damned certain she makes that call," I said, and hung up.

And stood there. Where do you go from here? I was *not* going to the airport, that was sure.

I was getting a little panicky. If I went to the airport it wouldn't help Doody, and I might get shot myself; if Scalzo could kill both of us he'd be clear, home free. But if I *didn't* go to the airport . . . I was damned if I did and damned if I didn't. By the time that call was put through to L.A. International, I *had to* find Doody. And seven-ten was only thirty-five minutes from now. What in hell could I do in thirty-five minutes? I didn't even know where to start.

It was a thousand to one against their being holed up at Scalzo's home, or any other place I'd be likely to check. Probably it would be somewhere in or near Los Angeles, or Hollywood — and I was still only a few miles from Hollywood Park in Inglewood.

But I couldn't stand here. I had to do something.

I had thirty-five minutes to find out where they were.

Find out — and get there.

I'd gunned the Cad down Manchester to Western, then swung left on Western, headed for Hollywood. So far I'd been stuck at only one red light and had made good time, but ten minutes were gone by the time I reached Wilshire Boulevard. The light there was red, and as I hit the brakes, something like a sudden small explosion went off in my head.

Thoughts had been tumbling in my mind as I drove. I'd been able to think of only two people I had a chance to find in a hurry who might know where Scalzo was. One was Dan Quick, but Scalzo would have thought of that too. Quick could even be with Scalzo now. The other was Matthew Wyndham, who lived in Beverly Hills, but it was a hundred to one against his knowing a thing. Even if by some freak chance he should know, I'd get nowhere asking him polite questions over the phone — and Beverly Hills was too far away to visit. Even from where I was now, it was a good half-hour drive, and it was 6:45 P.M. Only twenty-five minutes left.

There simply wasn't time. But thinking about phoning Wyndham closed a mental connection and made me remember that number Foster had dialed when I'd been with Doody in the Matador bar: 988-4584.

Since then I'd called it myself several times. Once when I'd been with Doody and three or four times the next morning — this morning, it had been, though it seemed a week ago. But there'd been other things to do, more urgent and important things. I hadn't even thought about that number for half a day.

Foster had been tailing me last night, I was pretty sure. Once I was settled with Doody at our table, he might simply have made an innocuous call. But, and a very big but it was, there was a good chance he'd been phoning his boss, in which case that number would be Scalzo's number. I knew it wasn't his home phone, but maybe it was another phone in the "somewhere" I had to find.

The light changed and I swung left into Wilshire, then off onto a side street and parked in a gas station next to its pay-phone booth. Ordinarily I would simply have phoned the police and told them what I wanted. But I knew by now the police would be eager to talk to me, and even though many of them are friends of mine, they would hardly be doing me favors until I'd answered a lot of questions.

So I fished Gabriel Rothstein's card from my wallet, and called him at home.

Boom, the familiar voice banged my ear. "Hello."

"Shell Scott, Mr. Rothstein. Listen close. I've got to know the name — and especially the address — of whoever has phone number 988-4584. It's probably unlisted. And I've got to find out fast."

"Where are you?"

"There's no time for that. Can you get me the information?"

"Just a moment." He put down the phone and was gone a minute or so. "I used another phone here. I'll be called back with the information. I stressed urgency. Now, where are you? I thought you'd be in jail by now."

"Jail? Hell, no. Not yet, anyway."

"Do you know the police are looking for you?"

"I guessed they might be. And it was an educated guess. How did you find out?"

"How did I find *out*? The story has been on every television newscast and radio broadcast. It is even in the newspapers now. Someone killed a man at Hollywood Park. In front of thousands of people. Was it actually you? If it truly was, this is catastrophic."

"Why catastrophic? What's so terrible . . ."

I was starting to understand. I'd been too busy worrying, about Doody, thinking, racing around, to consider fully what might by now have developed from this afternoon's episode at the track.

"Um," I said. "Yeah, it was me. Well, go on."

I heard him sigh. "Oh, there is more," he said. "Much more. Don't you understand? Only last Thursday, and also at Hollywood Park, a man was brutally murdered — but quietly, surreptitiously, by an unknown person or persons. Then two days later, today, on Saturday of all days, *you* run amuck and murder a man."

"I didn't run amuck, dammit. And I didn't *murder* anybody. I killed the sonofabitch, yes, but he had it coming — and if I'd been approximately one-fourth of a second slower, my brains would have been scattered over several square yards of Hollywood Park."

"I see." Silence for a few seconds. "There were some reports to that effect, reports alleging that the dead man did have a gun. But I fear few will believe them now. Frankly, Mr. Scott, I cannot understand how it is possible that you are still at liberty. The events at Hollywood Park have had an enormous impact locally. And certainly this will spread, be carried by the wire services nationally. You are wanted for questioning by the police on a charge of suspicion of murder. You are accused in addition of assault and battery. . . ." He paused again.

And during that pause it began filtering in that under the circumstances I probably should not be standing here in a glassed-in phone booth. And my sky-blue Cad, not unfamiliar to the police of seven counties, perhaps should not be parked out in the open a few feet away.

Rothstein continued, his voice vibrating like a high-pitched foghorn. "I am not yet aware of the source, but it has been divulged that you, Sheldon Scott, private investigator, were in my employ — even when you killed Mr. Deacon at Hollywood Park. That you were employed yesterday by Gabriel Rothstein to investigate Universal Electronics. That — Enough. My point is that I am being tarred with your brush. My previously cherished privacy has exploded into ghastly notoriety.

You were lucky to reach me. This phone has been ringing constantly. At this moment reporters are outside my home clamoring — demanding — to see me. I have been reviled, slandered, libeled."

"Look," I said, "I'm not exactly in the rosiest situation of *my* life at the moment — "

He broke in thunderously, "Whatever has occurred is of *your* doing — and *you* must undo it. The situation is extremely ugly now, but it can and will become uglier if allowed to continue. There is only one solution. You must without delay, before the rumors and half-truths and lies spread, confound them and bring this entire affair to a successful conclusion. You must prove your innocence of wrongdoing — if possible — and by so doing prove *my* innocence of wrongdoing. And by Heaven you must do it now, tonight."

Silence. Then he said, and his voice had as much vigor as had ever been in it, which was quite a lot: "Can you do it?"

"Well," I said. "Uh . . ."

"Can you do it?"

"Uh . . . Yes. Sure."

"How?"

"Beats me."

Silence again. "If you cannot do it, Mr. Scott, if you cannot deliver me from this appalling situation into which you have precipitated me, I swear to God I will ruin you. I can and if necessary will spend a million dollars to pursue and harass you. I will condemn you to a hell of my devising. Is that clear?"

"Yeah, it's clear," I said. "And quit threatening me. That's all I've had for most of this goddamn afternoon."

Just before he started to roar I heard the ring of a phone come over the wire. Clatter in the earpiece, silence for half a minute, then he was back. "That number is in the name of George M. Williams, of $1015^1/_2$ Laurel Way in Beverly Hills."

I grinned. Williams. Same address. The box next to Scalzo's at Hollywood Park. It made sense.

"Is that what you wanted?" Rothstein asked.

"That's what I wanted."

"Will it be of help?"

"Maybe, if I can get there — " I broke it off, glancing at my watch. "Oh, God. I have exactly seventeen minutes left. It's not enough."

It was 6:53 P.M. There wasn't nearly enough time to make it — even assuming, miraculously, that I wasn't collared by forty or fifty cops on the way.

Rothstein's voice broke in on my thoughts. "What do you mean, seventeen minutes?"

I hung up on him.

A block away a black-and-white police car flashed by on Wilshire. No, I damn well couldn't let the cops grab me. At least, not until long after those final minutes were used up.

I tried to calm myself down, get a grip on my thoughts. If George M. Williams was just a guy who went occasionally to the races, then there wasn't any hope. But if $1015^1/_2$ Laurel Way was Scalzo's hideout, then there was a little hope. Just a little.

Except that I had only seventeen minutes left and under ordinary circumstances it would take at least half an hour to get from here to Laurel Way in Beverly Hills — even breaking all the speed laws and running through stop lights, even risking a ticket, not to mention my neck.

Well, when you've eliminated the impossible, what remains is the possible. It was impossible for me to race through the city in my Cadillac. It was impossible, under ordinary circumstances, for me even to reach Beverly Hills in under half an hour.

But there was one way, just maybe, that made it possible.

So I took that way.

I drove three blocks and stole a police car.

Twenty

It took me two more minutes. Two vital minutes. But I got it. There was some luck, of course. It's said, though, that luck comes to those who are prepared for it. Maybe yes, maybe no — but I was sure as hell prepared to steal a locomotive if I had to.

The black-and-white L.A.P.D. buggy was parked outside a bar on Wilshire. It was empty, the engine running, calls coming over the police radio. One officer stood on the sidewalk just outside the door of the bar, looking in; his partner was probably inside checking on some kind of trouble.

Well, it was a certainty that soon they would both say the hell with that trouble and begin checking on trouble of their own. I was really charged up, the blood banging so hard through my body that it seemed ready to squirt out my pores. There must have been every kind of hormone and sauce and juice anywhere internally available steaming around among my corpuscles.

I left the Cad parked a yard behind the prowl car, ran to the police buggy and climbed in. I slapped the car in gear and dragged out, tires skidding and then biting. Maybe the officer yelled, I don't know. But I did. I yelled out of sheer excess of hormones, or pure nausea. God knows, but I yelled.

Then with the accelerator pedal jammed to the floor boards, I hit the red light and siren. No sense trying to sneak away now.

Fifteen minutes left. For a normal half-hour drive. And maybe nothing when — and if — I got there. But at least I had a chance with the accelerator down and siren clearing the way.

Six-fifty-six. Then six-fifty-seven. Two minutes gone; soon the call should be on the air. Here it came. I translated it between my ears as the dry facts and code crackled from my police radio: Police car stolen, proceeding west on Wilshire Boulevard, excessive speed, red light and siren. And — yeah, I guess that policeman had not only yelled but had been taking a pretty good look at me while yelling — "believed to be Sheldon Scott." Everything, even the license number — and, of course, it was a not invisible black-and-white car to begin with.

The voice was calm and controlled, but I could sense the flips between the lines. I could almost see the big, burly cops all over town straightening to snarling attention, hear the chorus of curses. All over town jaws bulging, arteries writhing like little boa constrictors. And Rothstein, I thought; wait'll he hears about this. Then I forced myself not to think about any of it.

Ahead of me, on both sides of the street, cars pulled to the side, clearing the way. A spot of red danced in the rearview mirror. Two or three blocks back, a police car was after me, red light flashing on its top. As I looked into the mirror, another radio car skidded around the corner only a block back, swerved, straightened out on Wilshire and came after me.

I swung right off Wilshire, over to Third, then over to Beverly and back toward Third again. A panel truck loomed ahead at an intersection and I hit the brakes, felt sudden strain in my arms. I yanked the wheel left and felt the car sway crazily as the tires slipped on the street. I missed the truck's rear bumper by inches, eased the steering wheel right and jammed the gas pedal down again, heart racing and the tight ball of sudden alarm still sticking in my throat.

Three minutes after seven. Seven minutes till Doody's call. Eight minutes, so far, of speeding down one street then another, sliding around corners and sometimes going north or even south but always moving west toward Beverly Hills. Sweat all over my body. Hands starting to cramp from the too-tight grip I had on the steering wheel. Mouth dry, stomach muscles tense almost to the point of pain.

Three red dots flickered in the rear-view mirror now; some I'd shaken, but others had taken their places. Suddenly there was one looming black-and-white, pulsing red, only yards away on my right. That's the danger in passing intersections with siren blaring — you can't hear the other siren if another police car or ambulance is careening toward you. It was a black-and-white prowl car, mate to mine, entering the intersection from my right at almost the same moment I did.

I don't think I did a thing. There wasn't time. I can't remember turning the steering wheel, but if the gas pedal wasn't on the floor boards before, it was as soon as I saw the other car. We came so close I thought a crash was inevitable, but before I knew it I was fifty yards past the intersection, still plummeting ahead. One quick glance at the rear-view mirror showed me the other car skidding sideways, slamming into the curb and rocking. But it stayed erect, didn't turn over.

On Third again I headed for Beverly Hills and just kept going. It was difficult to believe I hadn't been caught yet, hadn't been stopped. But then out of the muddle of my thoughts came an odd memory. I remembered reading about a man during the war who was hunted by twelve of the enemy on a deserted beach at night. In the darkness he joined them in their hunt — and got away with it too, until the leader of the enemy, having eliminated all possibilities but one, counted up to thirteen.

I started thinking I might make it, might really make it.

Unless a speeding prowl car was close enough so the pursuing officers could read my license number, it would be difficult for them to know whether my car was the fugitive's, or one of the police cars in hot pursuit of the fugitive. They might think I was chasing me. Maybe I'd make it; maybe . . .

The rest of that ride was a blur, sensation without thought. I hit Beverly Drive; I was in Beverly Hills. Skidded into it, raced across Sunset and past the Beverly Hills Hotel.

It was seven-eleven. I wasn't going to make it. I was a minute or two late — but still there had to be time for paging me at L.A. International, preparing to leave the house once they knew I wasn't going to answer the airport phone.

Then the sign: LAUREL WAY.

I braked, skidded through the left turn and hit the gas again. As I straightened out on Laurel Way I thought of something else. Scalzo, Doody, and whoever was with them might well be miles from here, not at $1015^1/_2$ Laurel Way at all. George M. Williams might be a ninety-year-old citizen who only went to the races twice a month. . . . But it was too late to worry about that now.

Seven-twelve; I was in the 1000 block. And, this close, after all the excitement and fear and shock of these past hours, all the soup floating around in my bloodstream had turned me on and off and very nearly inside out. There was a change in me, a literal change. There were probably chemicals lathering in my brain that had never before been farther up than my navel, and mentally I had traveled into a world of warped time and space, a kind of sugarplum Disneyland.

I felt light as a feather, almost floating, as if disembodied, able to walk through walls. There was a slight dizziness, a not unpleasant ringing in my ears, a kind of quivering alternation of heat and chill over my skin. I felt big as a house, strong as Gargantua, invincible — I was out of my mind.

Floating, I zoomed down the street. I thought of cutting the siren, decided not to. There was the house. A big white monster set back from the street on my left. A driveway alongside the house passed between two stone pillars, on the left one the number $1015^1/_2$. Between the pillars was a wrought-iron gate, closed, looped with chain.

I hugged the curb on the right of the street, slowing, tires screaming, swung left and headed for the iron gate. It flew at me like the skeleton of a great black bird. *Clang, crunch.* Then I was through, with an enormously musical scraping. Nothing to it; I didn't feel a thing.

I scrambled from the car, gun in my hand, bounced over spongy lawn toward the house. I sprinted forward, mind clicking like an abacus, eyes photographing every detail: Steps to a wide deck, a door — big door — beyond the steps, right of the door a huge plate-glass picture window beyond which I could see the interior of a dimly lighted room.

I clattered up the steps heading for the door, then my keen abacus-mind told me something: That door was an enormous thing made of something like foot-thick mangrove roots, with double doorknobs weighing approximately eighteen pounds apiece. If I ran into the thing it would knock me silly.

So, without any hesitation whatever, I veered and sprinted over the deck toward the picture window. That was it. That's the ticket, I thought dreamily: I'll leap through the window, just like they do in the movies. I plunged ahead, flipped my coat over my face, and leaped. I floated through the air. Floating, floating —

Blam!

It damn near knocked me unconscious. Like in the movies, huh? Well, I learned something; in movies they must use air and sound effects; they sure as hell don't use picture windows.

But I was going through — I was on my way — no turning back now. Soon I'd be in there with them and . . .

Oh, God, I thought. What if a little old lady is in there tatting doilies? If *that's* what was inside, there'd be screeches from every direction. The old gal would undoubtedly let out one horrendous squawk and die. And I'd get very ill indeed.

Glass was flying every which way. Shards and chunks and splinters of glass. I felt eleven million sharp shooting pains in my arms and hands and chest and — oh, hell, everywhere. It was like the moment at eighty thousand feet when you pull the ripcord and hang there expectantly, hopefully, which is to say horrified, the moment just before the chute opens — or doesn't.

What if my chute doesn't open? I thought.

What if those gangsters *are* in there, with ready submachine guns?

What if I don't ever get through this window?

Glass was flying, crashing, splintering. And sticking, plenty of that, all right.

Boy, this is hell, I thought.

A guy could get killed in all this glass. He could bleed to death in midair. Then: slap-slap, clunk. That was first one foot and then the other foot hitting the floor, and then my wounded rear end hitting the floor. My shoes had skidded on the carpet, or something on the carpet. Something? Glass!

Now I was skidding forward on my wounded rear end, but from suspense, wondering about all that glass on the floor. But I dug my heels into the carpet and, with a vigorous hop, was on my feet again.

And charging ahead.

Across the dimly lighted room. Another door, closed. They'd be in there. That's where they were. I steamed ahead, swung a shoulder around and thudded into the door. It splintered, crashed inward, and I flew through it, planted my feet and skidded.

In a blur I saw the faces floating. Scalzo, Hale, Scarlip — and Doody. They *were* in here.

And right then I came back from my sugarplum Disneyland.

Twenty-One

I came back all right. All the way.

The thread of euphoria snapped like a rubber band. The light, floating feeling disappeared and I felt unusual heaviness in my body. Even the ringing in my ears stopped and it was suddenly deathly quiet.

Doody was standing on the right of the room next to a table on which was a white phone. A yard from her was Hale, his mouth a hole of astonishment in his flat, fist-marked face. Near me on my left was the black-browed, black-eyed, black-hearted sonofabitch — Luke I'd heard him called — the scar on his upper lip like a flame against his pale face. And Scalzo, on my far left, stood across the room before an over-stuffed chair from which he must just have risen.

But none of them had guns in their hands.

And, automatically, I knew why. The siren. My deciding not to cut that siren was the reason they weren't ready to shoot whoever was crashing into the house. They'd probably expected a gang of policemen, not one man. Not me. Besides which, I'd been moving pretty fast.

But they didn't just stand there, either. In the same instant, they moved almost as one man. Scalzo slapped at his hip and Hale bent his knees, right hand darting under his coat. But nearest me was Luke and he sprang at me, not reaching for a gun, reaching for me.

The Colt was in my right hand and my thumb had already laid back the hammer, but Luke was almost on me. I turned toward him, raising my left elbow, pulling my hand in toward my chin and then whipping it out toward him, hand open, fingers straight and tense, thumb pulled back and cocked to tighten the ridge of muscle along my palm's edge.

My hand sliced under his chin and its edge thudded into his neck with the sound of a sandbag falling on a plank. It felt as if my hand had gone clear to the back of his head; I felt the gristle and cartilage of his windpipe silently crumple.

The gunshot and the impact were simultaneous. The bullet hit my left thigh and, oddly, felt like a cold blast against my skin. There was no pain, but the blow jarred me, spun me to my left. My knee bent and I felt myself falling sideways. Hale still held the gun before him, ready to fire again. Doody was too near him, too close — but she was dropping to the floor.

I fired and missed, landed on the carpet as Hale triggered his .45 again. The slug nipped at my coat but missed flesh. On my side, free hand against the floor, I aimed at Hale and fired. Scalzo was moving on my left, a blur, a flashing hand or arm in the edge of my vision, but I couldn't look toward him now. I squeezed the trigger again, knew I hit Hale, fired once more and this time saw his head jerk back.

On my left a gun cracked twice. Scalzo fired hurriedly, slower to get out his gun than Hale but quicker to pull the trigger; he must have jerked it, jerking the gun too — but he hit me. I felt the shock as metal bored through my right side.

In the time it took Scalzo to fire twice, I turned toward him and raised the Colt, felt more than saw the snubbed barrel lined up on his chest, and eased pressure down on the trigger. I kept the gun on him, kept pulling the trigger until the Colt's hammer clicked on an empty cartridge.

Scalzo pressed his hands to his middle, and blood poured from his throat. He swayed on his thick legs, large gray eyes staring. It looked as if he tried to step forward but couldn't move his legs. Then suddenly he thudded to the carpet and lay still, his shiny bald head toward me.

Doody got slowly to her feet and stood for several seconds with one hand at her throat. Then she ran across the room, knelt by me. "Shell, are you — are you hurt?"

I licked my lips. "I don't know. Not badly. I don't think so, anyway."

I heard sirens. For a moment I couldn't understand why there would be sirens so soon. But then I remembered. And how I remembered.

I felt over my body, winced when my fingers dug into a raw spot, gingerly tested my side. The worst place was from Hale's first shot, the one that had hit my thigh. Not only had it come closest to doing real damage, but — unlike Scalzo's smaller .38 — his gun had been a brutal Colt .45 automatic. The slug had missed bone, torn the flesh. I got to my feet. There was pain starting, but I could walk. The bullet from Scalzo's gun, the slug that had hit my side, had gone just under the skin, and the only other mark — except from all that glass, of course — was a shallow inch-long furrow on my neck.

"I'm all right," I said to Doody. "I won't go dancing for a while, but I'm all right."

"Thank God." She swallowed. "They . . . they were going to kill me. They *really* were. It's incredible . . ." She stared past me, lovely face still shocked and pale.

Outside was eerie blending of wails that meant at least two or three sirens, maybe more. A not unpleasant sound for a change. Almost music. Let them come, I thought. But with the thought was something else, a vague uneasiness I couldn't pin down, a small cold spot in my brain.

That queer little cold spot grew larger. It seemed to happen every time I thought about cops. They were going to give me a very rough time, I knew, but I could handle it now because I could explain . . . everything . . .

The cold spot was now not in my brain, it was my brain. It filled my skull, drooled down my spine.

"Oh," I said. It was a very soft sound.

"What's the matter, Shell?"

I didn't answer. I looked at the bodies. I went over to them, hunted for pulses, did not find any pulses. Not even in scarlipped Luke. My hand had crushed his neck, trachea, bone, and cartilage, sealed his throat with gristle. He was dead. So were Scalzo and Hale. I found a chair, sank into it.

"*Please*, Shell, what's *wrong?*"

"Everything." I sighed. "About a thousand cops are going to stampede in here soon. In a minute or two, maybe in seconds. And — well, you've been out of touch. At the moment the entire Los Angeles Police Department, and an appreciable percentage of local voters, would cast their ballots to dissolve me in caustic solutions. They desire to electrocute me, hang me, gas me, skin me alive."

"But isn't everything all right now?"

"Not . . . quite." I looked around at the bodies. "No, not quite. Doody, for me to convince those who need convincing, I will need much more than my simple statement and a lot of dead bodies. Especially when I made the bodies dead. Even with what you can say about Luke's snatching you, that is not enough; Luke, you see, is a corpse. Your unsupported word is not enough. *My* unsupported word is not enough, not by a long shot."

"I don't understand."

"You will."

The sirens sounded as if they were inside the house now. A lot of sirens. I was coming unglued. "Doody, I don't even know about Ryder — your dad — the embezzlement . . . and *that's* what I was hired to find out in the first place. They thought I went too far when I plugged Deke at Hollypark, but *now. . ."*

"But they were going to kill me, Shell. They tried to kill you."

"You tell the cops that. *You* tell them. . . ."

Life stirred. My brain thawed a little.

"Yeah, Doody," I said more briskly, "you do that." I stood up. "And tell it good, because I won't be here. I hope."

"You're *leaving?*"

"Probably not, but I'm going to give it a try. After what has already happened — well, let's say it is barely within the realm of the possible."

Sirens moaned in front of the house. Big feet would soon be bouncing over the lawn, and probably big clubs would soon be bouncing over my head.

"Tell the cops everything you know," I said rapidly. "It should at least help prepare them for my tale if I get a chance to tell it." I looked down at her. "So, Doody, tell it good, and I'll try to wrap up the rest of it. Somehow."

She was close to me, almost touching me, those unforgettable eyes fringed with lashes like black lace, lips moistly gleaming.

Came a great hammering and banging on the door.

"Shell," Doody said, "I don't really understand. But you'll do it. I know you will."

Well, when a woman with a face like that and a body like that says something like that, when she looks up at you with her eyes shining, and when she speaks like that in a voice that could split your toenails — what do you do?

Why, you kiss her, of course. You pull her close, feel her body pressed against you, molded to you, warm and soft and alive, and, yes, you kiss her.

Sure, more sirens were swelling, there was banging on the door, there was no time. . . .

But, friend, for that, even when there's no time, I'll take time. The police could have been pouring through the doors and windows, syndicate to the left of me, Mafia to the right of me, the devil himself behind me volleying and thundering — and I would *still* have kissed her.

It would have been worth it, too. It was. I don't know how long the kiss lasted. I'd say just long enough. It started out spectacular and improved steadily. This, after all, was not the batty blonde I'd once thought her, but a brilliant tomato who spoke seven languages, and she kissed me in all those seven languages, then in Esperanto.

Man, the lips! They were lips like wine — like booze! — like burning brandy, lips with lightning in them. They were lips that could ignite dry kindling, a whole mouthful of lips, a universe of osculatorching, an exploding pucker — words failed me, but my lips kept on succeeding.

It ended only when the door out front crashed inward. Yeah, the door — and here I'd opened the window for them.

But that was my signal: Go. I went.

I turned and floated through the room, out the back door, pausing to open it instead of gaily knocking it off its hinges, and soared into the night. So there were ten thousand cops out there. Mafia, syndicate. Devil, all kinds of creeps — who cared? Nothing would stop me now. The rest of this would be a breeze.

I knew it would be. It was.

Twenty-Two

The window was open. I slid it all the way up and pulled myself through and inside.

This was Matthew Wyndham's home in Beverly Hills. Two hours had passed since I'd left Doody and started running.

I'd run out the back door, past a swimming pool, through landscaped grounds, over a wall, and just kept going for two more blocks in the same direction. Then I saw the first prowl car — I'd heard it coming, siren bansheeing, and was prone behind a hedge when it went by. Another time I hid behind a tree, and once trotted into somebody's back yard. I hadn't made it all the way to Wyndham's on foot, for after hiding briefly in that back yard I let myself into somebody's darkened house.

The only trouble I had was finding the phone. But I found it, phoned a taxi agency in Hollywood, and asked for a particular driver. He was a man I'd done a favor for in time past, a man who did not love the law but did like me, and therefore wouldn't tip the law. I left word for him to call and stood for twenty minutes, silently, hand on the phone.

When it rang, I didn't have to pick the receiver off fast to still the sound. I jumped six inches in the air and the phone came up with me after hardly a *ting*. I told him where to pick me up, and climbed into his cab when he showed. He left me at Wyndham's and I was on my own again.

There were no cops at Wyndham's. Why should there be? He wasn't a crook. He was the respectable president of Universal Electronics; he even belonged to the Beverly Club.

I visited three rooms upstairs and turned on three sets of lights before I found his bedroom. I was rather pleased that I hadn't stumbled into Mrs. Wyndham's bedroom. But I was even more pleased to find Wyndham in his bed.

In bed, yes. But not asleep. I imagine that before I turned on the light he'd been lying there in the darkness, his eyes staring. Well, after today — and all the rest of it — I could understand why.

I shut the door behind me, walked toward the bed. He rose to a sitting position and looked at me as if I were Death, alive and striding toward him. He stared, and choking sounds gurgled from his throat.

Understandably, too. To begin with, it was I, it was Shell Scott, whom he did not relish seeing ever again in the first place. And in the second place I was all over blood, hastily and sloppily bandaged, limping, clothes torn, face somewhat unpleasant. And, too, I had a gun, my now empty Colt, in my hand.

I must have looked pretty gruesome to Matthew Wyndham, virtually dismembered, certainly ghostly. Not exactly the ghost of Christmas past, maybe Halloween behind, but nothing encouraging to him. He let out his breath with a sigh and sort of collapsed.

"Hello again, Matthew," I said softly.

More gurgling sounds.

I sat on the edge of the bed and my weight pushed it down. He started to roll toward me and shrank away. I stuck my empty gun in front of his right eye and thumbed back the hammer. He closed his eyes and waited. Just waited.

"I'm not going to kill you, Matthew," I said. "I'm going to talk to you. More important, you're going to talk to me."

After a while he opened his eyes.

I said, "Isn't that right?" and put the gun away.

He licked his lips, eventually got a word out. "Yes . . . yes . . ."

"You knew they were going to kill me today, didn't you?"

He shivered. "Yes, I knew," he said. "I knew they meant to."

"As they killed John Kay."

He nodded, but didn't speak.

"I'll tell you how it was. You tell me what I miss. Kay suspected, as I did, that you were meeting Scalzo somewhere, though apparently nobody had seen you two together. Kay knew, or learned, that you met at the track, and Thursday, before you or Scalzo arrived, he planted a transmitter — a microphone — in the box you used. Somehow

Scalzo found out about it and sent one or two of his hoods to take care of Kay."

I stopped and waited and he spoke without urging.

"Yes. Axel — Scalzo — saw Kay, and noticed something that disturbed him. He asked me if Kay had worn a hearing aid when he'd visited me in my office and I told him no, he hadn't. That was all I did. That was all." He stopped briefly. "Scalzo spoke to the one called Hale. I don't know what he said. Hale looked around in their box, then in mine, and found — I don't know what it was."

"I do."

"Then Hale and another man walked up to Kay. That's all I know."

"Sure. Who was the other man? Guy with a scar on his lip?"

"No, Deacon. Deke."

So Hale and Deke had done the actual killing of Kay. On Scalzo's order, of course. Well, all three of the bastards were dead. I wasn't sorry.

"The last time we talked, you told me you didn't know Ardis Ames." When I said her name, he twitched a little. "I know better," I said. "I know she's in Fairlawn Cemetery. Want to tell me about it?"

His mouth twisted, but he didn't speak.

"Did you kill her?" I asked.

"No. She's dead, but I . . . didn't kill her." He swallowed. "I loved her."

It got to me a little. He wasn't lying; there was too much emotion and quiet conviction, too much raw aching in his voice.

"Who did kill her?"

"No one. Or I suppose I did, in a way."

He stopped and I waited silently.

"She — she was going to have my child. But, well, it was out of the question, impossible. There was an abortion, but too late. She died."

"Uh-huh. It figures."

He had been looking at his hands. But when I spoke, he turned his face toward me. "What do you mean?"

"Well, how do you . . ." I started over. "Did someone *tell* you she was dead?"

"No. I saw her."

That jolted me. "Saw her? Where?"

"In the viewing room at Fairlawn. She had died during the night. I looked at her. . . ." He was staring at his hands again. "I touched her cold breast. She was dead, Ardis was dead." His voice was barely audible and his lips quivered. His chest rose and fell as he sighed. "I put flowers on her grave," he said, and there were real tears in his eyes.

I hated to keep pushing it, but I had to know it all. And I'd just had another thought. I didn't believe, of course, that Ardis had died as the result of an abortion. But Scalzo was such a complete monster he might himself have killed her, or had her killed, because a really dead woman would serve his purpose better.

But I decided to go at it from an angle. "Just what did Scalzo have on you?" I asked him.

And the door opened behind me.

I swung around. It was butler-chopped Mrs. Wyndham. She had on a nightgown that, if universally worn, would put a severe crimp in the human race. I won't describe it. I don't like describing that sort of thing. But, briefly, it looked as if she were moulting.

"What is the meaning of this?" she bellowed. "What is the mean — hah!"

She'd just gotten a good look at me.

She reeled back a step, flinging a hand up, perhaps to shield her eyes. A killer was not only loose, but here in the house. Then she spun about. "Police!" she cried, as if that alone would bring them.

I looked at Wyndham. "I can stop her. But you'd better do it. Do it or listen to me tell her the tale. She'll know soon enough, but move, mister, or she'll know it now."

His face was ashen. He sat frozen for a moment, then his jaw hardened. He got an almost fierce look on his face and, as I stood up, he swung out of bed.

Wearing the bottom half of purple pajamas, he thumped barefoot across the room to the door. "Maude!" he yelled. "*Maude!*"

She cackled something and he shouted, "*Shut up!*" Believe me, she screamed. Those two words, I guess, were more shocking than the sight of me, dying on Matthew's bed. "Come here," Wyndham said. "Come here, damn you."

I was seeing history in the making.

I heard Maude approaching her husband on staggering feet. He spoke to her in a tone so low I couldn't hear the words. But I heard one more small scream from Mrs. Wyndham. Then footsteps, a door slamming.

Wyndham came back in. Shoulders high, step firm, teeth firmly together.

"O.K.," I said. "Nice work. Now let's continue. Scalzo got his hooks in you, and after you'd looted your company for payoff money, and then more and more payoff money, you saw exposure around the corner. So you started framing Ryder Tangier to get off the hook. Temporarily, that is. Only you're still on the blackmail hook, and it's in even deeper now, since Scalzo not only has the original dirt on you but also knows about your embezzlement and the framing of Tangier as well. Did I miss anything?"

"That's preposterous," he said. "I was not blackmailed, and I did not steal any money. I feel sorry for Ryder. But he is guilty."

He sat on the edge of the bed. Shoulders high, teeth firmly together.

"Now look," I said. "O.K., you're a hero. You should have done it before. It would probably have prevented a lot of trouble. But don't let it go to your head. Now spill it, Wyndham."

He sat there, shoulders high, and so on.

I hated to do it, even to him. But he'd asked for it. I said, "Don't you know yet that Dr. Noble isn't a doctor?"

It stuck him pretty good. At least his teeth came apart. I waited for his answer, but there could be only one answer. If he had known who Noble really was, he certainly would not have introduced him to me at the Beverly Club as Dr. Noble, nor would he have so innocently informed me that the doctor's office was in the Western Insurance Building. He'd thought he was telling me the innocuous truth.

Finally Wyndham said, "Not a doctor?"

I said, "He is one of the slickest confidence men in the state of California, at least, and among his fellow felons he is known as Dandy Dan Quick."

"That's impossible."

"Prepare yourself," I said. "Because you're going to see the impossible."

We parked in front of the Angeles-Sands and went inside as fast as I could force Wyndham to move.

There was reason for hurry. There were sirens warbling all over the place. Wyndham had dressed with speed and we'd driven through town in his big black Cadillac, he at the wheel and the back seat occupied only by me, me and my empty gun. On our drive it became evident that the police were still busy. I was popular tonight; I was really wanted. But nobody had better try stopping me now, I thought. Not this close.

We went up to the third floor in the elevator, down the hall to 308, and knocked.

Footsteps. The door opened. It wasn't Dandy Dan, but Mrs. Quick, the Bikini-bottom blonde with the supercharged top. This time she was wearing a robe that hid everything below her face.

But it was her face at the moment that counted. She looked at Matthew Wyndham, past him to me, then at Wyndham again. She shrugged, sighed, then said to Wyndham:

"Hello, you fat old bastard."

"My God," he said. *"My God!"* And fainted dead away.

"Well, Ardis," I said, "you could at least help me drag him in. The jig, as they say, is up."

She let the robe fall open. "Couldn't we talk this over — "

I laughed. "Not a chance, baby. So turn off the heat. You're dead."

Twenty-Three

Wyndham lay on a couch with his mouth open, still out. Ardis — actually the real Mrs. Dan Quick, if you're interested in these insights into the criminal character — sat beside me on a divan. Dan was out in some bar somewhere, she said. I didn't much care if he was or not; I didn't really need him now.

Mrs. Quick — Ardis to me — knowing she had been irrevocably stabbed, was spilling all without restraint. She knew it would soon come from Wyndham anyway.

She told me how, working for Axel Scalzo, she and Dan had slowly and expertly built the con around Wyndham, wound him up tight, bled him for money; how after her "death" the fake Dr. Noble had further bled him, in order to get the hooks in deeper and deeper, and then "turned him over" to Scalzo.

"Matt didn't even let out a peep," she said. "Dan could have turned him over to Lassie and he'd have started barking."

"So at that point Wyndham thought only Scalzo and Dan knew about his sinful relations with you, right?" She nodded and I said, "I suppose Dan visited Wyndham in his office this week because John Kay had started nosing around?"

"Yes, Kay hit Matt's office last Friday and scared him half to death. When Matt told Axel about it over the weekend, all shook up, Axel had Dan drop in on him a couple times to cool him down, keep him in line. You know, remind him of dear dead Ardis and so on."

She didn't know for sure, but I figured Kay must have told Wyndham he was working for Gabriel Rothstein. There'd been no murder at that time, and thus less reason for secrecy and caution.

149

Which would explain why hoods had been watching Rothstein's office — especially after Kay was killed.

"How did you make Wyndham believe you were dead?" I asked her.

"By that time he would have believed Scrooge was Santa Claus. We had him so tight we could have sent him to Alaska for ice cubes. I just stretched out on a slab, naked, and he took one gawk and started blubbering. 'Ardis, dear Ardis, she's gone, I've killed her.' And things you wouldn't believe."

"I'd believe them." I pulled an ear. That was one thing I could rub without starting blood flowing again. "What I can't believe is that your breasts were cold when he touched you."

"Thanks lots," she said without conviction. "Dan rubbed me with ice. It even made me look deader. I damn near froze." She shook her bead. "You know. Matt grabbed one and I thought he was going to pull it off. 'dead!' he yells. I just about came to life right then, and that would have fixed it. It was like getting tickled in church. I almost busted to keep from laughing."

"Yeah, hilarious," I said.

And right then Matthew Wyndham stirred, sat up, and looked at Ardis Ames, his risen love, with ashes in his eyes. Slowly his chest heaved from his labored breathing. He stared. Then he got to his feet, walked to her, and dropped to his knees. He took one of her hands in both of his, felt the warm flesh, and looked up at her face.

"Ardis," he said. "Ardis. Thank God."

Ardis Ames — Mrs. Dandy Dan Quick — looked at me and jabbed a thumb at Wyndham. "Get him," she said.

Yes, that's the way it is with con men — and women.

They're usually lovely people, charming, intelligent, quick to laughter — with tongues of gold-plated brass and the conscience of hell's harlots. They can take your money, and break your heart, and laugh, and laugh, and laugh. While they count your money. Oh, they laugh a lot, all right. They're happy sonsof-bitches.

We sat in silence, each of us with our individual thoughts. After a minute or two I said to Wyndham, "I suppose you'll tell me now. Right, Mr. Wyndham?"

He nodded briskly. Strange, maybe, but he looked almost happy. "Yes, Mr. Scott, I'll tell it all."

And with that I prepared to face the music.

So I called the cops, and they arrived very soon. You wouldn't believe how soon. . . .

Twenty-Four

Of course, they had to put me in jail.

It was only for three days, but I guess I was lucky it wasn't life. Actually, it wasn't the slammer, but the prison ward of General Hospital. And, frankly, I didn't mind at all.

They estimated that of the approximately six quarts of blood in a human body, I had lost, through spurting and seepage and various other ingenious means, no less than eight gallons. That's what they said, but they were probably joshing me a bit.

On the third day, Gabriel Rothstein visited me in the hospital ward and he was a man renewed, revitalized, rejuvenated. I guess when he was feeling good he talked a little louder than usual, and while his voice didn't actually chip plaster, it brought patients back from the edge of the next world, which is pretty far away. He was happy for many reasons — one of which was that he was making money. After all, there's nothing wrong with making lots and lots of money; it's all in *how* you make it. See: Axel Scalzo, Wyndham, Dandy Dan and Mrs. Quick.

Universal Electronics stock had moved a point higher on the American Exchange Monday morning. Each day since then it had climbed upward, and when it was official that Ryder Tangier — proved innocent by Wyndham's detailed confession — was being released from San Quentin and would return to UE, his remarkable noodle teeming with genius-type inventions and products and projects, the stock took a spurt that made even me start thinking of yachts.

Rothstein happily offered me more stock, more money, which I refused. I did, however, accept his offer to pay any unusual expenses which I had incurred in the course of my investigation. He was delighted to do it, but no more delighted than I, since some of those expenses were unusually unusual. He settled happily with everybody, including citizens whose cars or property had been stolen or scraped, such as cops.

The annual stockholders' meeting, held on Monday, must have been dandy. I wasn't there, but Rothstein was and told me about it. By then the news was all over town that "gangsters and hoodlums" had been boring into the company and trying to win control of UE.

That, of course, had been Axel Scalzo's design from the beginning, why he'd used Mr. and Mrs. Dandy Dan to get his hooks into UE's president, why he'd been buying stock himself and through fronts. Scalzo hadn't anticipated Wyndham's stealing — to conceal from his own wife, and their joint accounts, the fact that he was being bled for thousands — but crooks, whether gambling for pennies or millions, always make some kind of mistake, and Scalzo had made several.

At any rate, it was thought for a while that the stockholders' meeting might have to be held in the L.A. Coliseum, but they finally found a hall big enough to seat the gang that showed up. The story was told, and after some confusion, the share owners went away convinced UE's future was now brighter than ever. Gabriel Rothstein himself told them so — and that I wish I could have heard.

So the score was:

Dead: Axel Scalzo, Hale, Deke, Luke, Foster.

Jailed: Matthew Wyndham, Dandy Dan, Mrs. Quick, miscellaneous hoods and connivers.

Freed: Ryder Tangier.

Richer: Gabriel Rothstein.

Wiser: Mrs. Matthew Wyndham, among others.

Still Sick: Eddy Sly.

Pooped: Me.

And that was about it. No, I haven't forgotten Julie Tangier. I haven't forgotten Doody. Forgotten? Me?

It was a week after Thunder Boy had won the seventh race — the one we hadn't bet on, when I'd finally picked a a winner. Another Saturday. Or, rather, Saturday night. I was no longer pooped. On the contrary, I was full of beans. Feeling great. As for my wounds and bullet holes, there were still a few twinges, but, as you may have suspected, I heal fast.

So Doody and I had gone out amongst 'em, out on the town. She'd had the glad reunion with her father, Ryder Tangier; all the duties were done, and it was one of those nights when everything's right, when you're really glad to be alive. We'd eaten at an expensive restaurant where the headwaiter kidnaped the tables and held them for ransom, dinner complete with cocktails and wine and flaming things, then dancing, strolling, riding.

Riding in the Cad with the top down, along the Hollywood Freeway, into Vine, down North Rossmore, and — imagine! There's the Spartan Apartment Hotel. How about that?

In my apartment Doody glared at Amelia, smiled at the fish, burned me with her eyes. We sat on the oversize chocolate-brown divan, she curled in a corner, me with my feet propped on a leather hassock. The drinks were Scotch-and-soda for her, bourbon-and-water for me.

We talked about the evening, about the case, a little of everything.

"Here's a thought," I said. "Now that I no longer fear the gas chamber — and we're both unemployed — why don't we take off on a little cruise? Gabriel Rothstein's planning a vacation in Acapulco — for his nerves. And he's invited us to join him on 'The Golden Bull,' his zillionaire-size yacht."

"Invited us?"

"Well, me. But I can ask the lady of my choice. Let's see, there's Carmen — no, not Carmen. She goes wild when the sun comes up. Ah, there's — "

"There's me."

"I don't know. You're too bright. You'd probably want to talk to me in Greek."

"I could whisper to you in Greek, Or" — she smiled — "or I could be Doody."

I laughed. "That might do it. Doody speaks only one language. *My* language."

"So does Julie," she said quietly. Then she smiled. "You're nobody's fool, Shell. But that night when I was with Scalzo and those awful men I thought he'd finally outwitted you. He had, all right — like Custer outwitted the Indians. When you came through that door I thought my heart would stop."

"So did I — mine, I mean. The truth is, I didn't really want to be there, but in a moment of weakness I volunteered."

"You'll always volunteer, Shell. That's one of the things I like about you. You're a nut."

"Now you're talking."

"So come over here and sit by me."

"I've been wounded, you know."

"You only *think* you've been wounded." She smiled a slow smile. Then — that magic again. The eyes a little wider, mouth a bit more rounded, voice thinner, higher in the scale.

"Shellie," she said sweetly. "You're ordered to volunteer again."

Eyes that sizzled and lips like flaming puckers — or unforgettable eyes fringed with lashes like lace, voice soft and lips honey-sweet — Julie or Doody, brilliant or batty, it made no difference. "Shellie. . . ."

The rest is none of your business. Suffice to say — as she might have said — a word to the wise is efficient: I saw my Doody, and I did it.

Biography

Richard Prather

Richard Prather is the author of the world famous Shell Scott detective series, which has over 40,000,000 copies in print in the U.S. and many millions more in hundreds of foreign-language editions. In 1986 he was awarded the Private Eye Writers of America's Life Achievement Award for his contributions to the detective genre. He and his wife, Tina, live among the beautiful Red Rocks of Sedona, Arizona. He enjoys organic gardening, gin on the rocks, and golf. He collects books on several different life-enriching subjects and occasionally re-reads his own books with huge enjoyment, especially STRIP FOR MURDER.

Printed in the United States
5943